Trail of the Sacred Wolf

An Arizona White Mountain Adventure

Daniel Scott Deublein

ISBN: 979-8-218-63202-8

Disclaimer

This is a work of fiction. Any names, characters, businesses, organizations, places, events, or incidents are either the product of the author's imagination or used in a fictitious manner. Any resemblance to actual persons, living or dead, or events is coincidental. The author has made every effort to ensure accuracy regarding locations, historical references, and factual details; however, creative liberties have been taken for storytelling. No part of this book is intended to defame, misrepresent, or infringe upon real individuals or entities.

Dedication

To those who read *Trail of the Forgotten Grizzly,* it was your support, enthusiasm, and kind words that gave me the courage to embark on another adventure.

This book exists because of you.

Acknowledgment

To the readers of *Trail of the Forgotten Grizzly,* your support and enthusiasm have brought this story to life and turned it into a series – thank you!

To my wife, whose unwavering support, keen editorial eye, and endless encouragement made this book possible.

To everyone who offered feedback, shared your thoughts, and provided unwavering support, thank you for being a partner in this journey.

In today's ever-changing world of technology, I've used AI as an assistant in my writing process. But every word, idea, and vision on these pages stems from my own creativity.

And to those who live and serve in the White Mountains of Arizona, you are the true guardians of this land. Your dedication and stewardship ensure its beauty and spirit will endure for future generations.

With heartfelt appreciation,

Daniel Scott Deublein

About the Author

Daniel Scott Deublein, a native of Show Low, Arizona, continues his journey as an author with *Trail of the Sacred Wolf*, the second novel in his White Mountain Adventure series. Following the success of *Trail of the Forgotten Grizzly*, he remains committed to weaving stories that capture the untamed beauty and rugged spirit of the Arizona wilderness.

A former actor known for roles such as Ben Swift on *Beverly Hills, 90210,* Daniel transitioned from Hollywood to a medical career, earning a Master of Science Degree from Des Moines University and becoming a board-certified Physician Associate. In retirement, he remains dedicated to providing medical care to the remote villages of Alaska.

Now settled in Greer, Arizona, where he and his wife have built their log home, Daniel draws inspiration from the surrounding area. His passion for storytelling extends beyond novels—his award-winning short film *Rooted in Arizona* showcases his love for the land and its history. As an advocate for conservation, he remains committed to preserving the Arizona White Mountains for future generations.

Preface

Dear Readers,

I didn't initially plan to write this second book, but your feedback and enthusiasm for my first book inspired me to continue writing and transform this story into a series. I'm truly grateful for your support.

As a native of the White Mountains of Arizona, I am continuously inspired by what I believe is the most beautiful part of the state. These mountains, their history, and their people have shaped me in ways I never fully appreciated until I embarked on the journey to commit this story to paper.

My connection to the Apache Tribe runs deep. My father owned Horseshoe Pizza in Whiteriver for many years, and I spent my weekends working there while in school. During that time, I formed friendships and gained a deeper understanding of Apache culture – their strong bond with the land and their spiritual connection to these mountains. I have done my best to weave those elements into this book, honoring their wisdom and profound respect for nature.

Writing **Trail of the Sacred Wolf** has been an incredible experience. This story explores themes close to my heart—our bond with the land, the power of heritage, and the responsibility we all share in protecting these mountains.

This book is more than just a story – it carries an important message and is a stark reminder of how fragile this land is. One careless mistake could take it all away.

If you cherish these mountains as I do, please do your part to care for them. Respect the land and its wildlife so future generations can experience this beauty as we have.

As I said in my first book, I'm not an expert at anything. I'd call myself a below-average author and a pretty good Physician Associate. While I am sure I've made some mistakes in my writing, I hope this book connects with you.

Keep it Wild,

Daniel Scott Deublein

Contents

I: Untamed Grace

ON THE SHOULDER OF HIGHWAY 260, near Horseshoe Lake, a quiet gathering of tourists pointed their phones towards the distance. In the twilight, Mount Baldy stood like a silent sentinel; its peak brushed in light snow. Wild horses grazing in the foreground, their sleek and powerful forms moving harmoniously along the tree line, unaware of the tourists marveling at them.

The air was crisp as sunlight filtered down through the golden aspen, casting an amber glow across the scene. Leaves were stirring in a faint breeze, and the call of an Osprey could be heard deep within the forest.

A crack, a sharp one, and a sudden one that split the air and echoed through the trees. It sent birds scattering throughout the sky. The unmistakable sound of a gunshot ripped through the serenity and froze the tourists in their tracks. Before anyone could react, two more shots had been fired, each sharper than the first.

One of the wild horses, a gray mustang with a thick, proud mane, jerked forward as a bullet tore through its chest. Eyes wide with terror, staggering sideways as his legs folded beneath him. Then, a chestnut mare quickly reared up beside him, nostrils flaring in panic, and then a bullet found her, too. The mare's body collapsed beside the mustang, her legs twitching in the final spasms of life.

Gasps turned to screams as the tourists scrambled backward, capturing the grisly scene on their phones. The metallic tang of blood now tainted the rich smell of pine and soil as the horses lay crumpled upon the ground. Behind the trees, an old, rusty blue truck roared to life. Mud flew as its tires spun against the soil, speeding off with a throaty growl and disappearing into the distance. People quickly scrambled to catch a glimpse of the license plate, shouting descriptions to one another in panicked voices.

"Did anyone get the plate number?" a woman cried.

"It was old - rusted out! Dark blue!" shouted another.

"I… I think it was something with a 'B' or an '8'—*I don't know!*"

A man in a red windbreaker, hands trembling, raised his phone to snap a quick picture of the retreating vehicle, but it was already a fading speck in the distance, disappearing down the forest road as if swallowed by the trees.

The tourists stood paralyzed, staring at the aftermath. Everything was still - the only motion was the slow trickle of blood seeping into the damp soil. A woman pressed her hand to her mouth, her eyes tearful. "How could anyone…?"

A young boy clung to his mother's leg, his face buried in her side, scared yet unable to look away. His mother stroked his hair, her face pale as she whispered, "It's okay, honey. Just… don't look."

The man in the red windbreaker stared at the fallen horses, slowly shaking his head. "This isn't right," he muttered, barely above a whisper. "These animals…they did nothing wrong."

Around him, the others nodded numbly.

Suddenly, a horn cut through the tense silence. A silver truck bearing the Arizona Game and Fish Department logo pulled up to the scene; its engine cut off with a low rumble. The door opened and out stepped Ethan Wagner, a now-established game warden. His gaze was steady upon the dead horses, but his attention darted back as he moved through the crowd. He reached a young woman, her arm stretched out with her cell phone.

"Miss," he said, his voice soft but clear. "Are you okay? Did you happen to capture anything on your phone?" He nodded toward her screen with a slight smile. "We could use anything you got."

The woman blinked, nodding slowly as her grip on her cell phone loosened slightly. "I...yes, I think so." she stammered. "It all happened so fast. I think I was able to get the truck." She handed Ethan her phone.

"Part of the truck is better than no truck." Ethan smiled, helping to relieve the tension. He swiped through her photos, his expression shifting slightly as he studied a blurry shot of a blue truck speeding away.

"Folks, I'm Ethan Wagner with Arizona Game and Fish," he called out, raising his voice to address everyone. "I'm here to figure out what happened, but I'll need your help. If anyone else has any photos or videos, a look at the truck's occupants, or any other information, please let me know."

As murmurs rippled through the group, a second vehicle approached, and a woman stepped out; her expression was an odd mix of calm and sorrow. She moved past the tourists and towards the fallen horses, kneeling beside the mustang to inspect its injuries. She reached out, fingers light but steady as she traced the edge of the bullet hole in the horse's chest.

Ethan joined her, crouching down as he spoke quietly. "Not how either of us wanted to end our day, is it?"

She looked up with sadness flickering in her eyes. "Whoever did this knew exactly what they were doing. These weren't stray shots."

"I agree," he replied grimly, running a hand over his jaw. "Someone's idea of a sick thrill."

He glanced at the boy clinging to his mother, his face pressed against her leg, his eyes wide with fear and confusion. Ethan's demeanor softened as he approached the young boy.

"Hey, buddy," he said gently. "You're being so brave. I'm here to make sure everyone's safe, alright?" The boy looked up at him and nodded with relief. His mother mouthed a quiet *'thank you,'* and Ethan gave her a quick nod before turning his attention to the woman investigating the horses.

"Anything to add to the report, Maria?" he asked, studying her as she continued her examination.

Maria's expression grew thoughtful, her brows furrowing as she touched the horse's coat near the wound. "Close-range shots. Whoever did this was stalking these horses, waiting for the right moment." She glanced up at him, her gaze steady. "This was all planned, Ethan."

He exhaled sharply. "Planned or not, they won't get away with it."

His hand moved to rest on his hip, where his radio was clipped. "Makes it worse somehow, doesn't it?" he said softly, the usual lightness in his tone gone. He looked over the scene again, his eyes narrowed as he took in the bloodstained ground and the darkening shadows stretched across the earth as the sun continued to sink.

One of the individuals, an older man with a scruffy beard and a well-worn Show Low Cougars baseball cap, stepped forward and cleared his throat nervously. "I, uh, I saw the truck too. Looked like an old pickup to me. Had a busted taillight on the right."

Ethan turned, nodding in appreciation. "Thank you, sir. That is very helpful."

A few more voices joined in, adding details about the unfortunate incident, and Ethan's sharp gaze moved between them, absorbing each detail. Maria moved over to the chestnut mare, her fingers brushing along its mane, her face softening as she murmured something under her breath.

Ethan walked over to her, lowering his voice. "You alright?"

Maria looked up, her expression steady but tinged with a sadness that was hard to hide. "I hate seeing them like this, Ethan. These animals didn't deserve this." She hesitated, glancing around to ensure the tourists were out of earshot, then lowered her voice further. "This is the third shooting this year, Ethan."

Ethan nodded, his expression softening. "It's ugly. No two ways about it." He briefly touched her shoulder, giving it a reassuring squeeze. "We'll get to the bottom of it. Whoever did this isn't gonna get away with it. Not on our watch."

After gathering the last details, Ethan turned to the crowd, his voice firm. "Thank you for your help. We're taking seriously any details, no matter how small, that could be useful. If you recall any details later, please get in touch with us at Arizona Game and Fish. We'll see that justice is done," he said, handing out his business card.

A woman in a green puffy jacket raised her hand, her voice trembling slightly. "I saw the truck parked off the road just a little before the shots....it was sort of visible from the hiking trail I was on. I thought it was suspicious... there aren't any turn-offs around there, and they just looked like they were up to something."

Ethan gave her a reassuring nod. "That's exactly the kind of details we need. Thank you, ma'am. Anyone else?"

He looked around at the others who were either prodding their memories or looking around in slight bewilderment. His face shifted to a serious expression once more. "Alright then, folks. Again, do not worry; the Department will make sure this is handled, and we appreciate your cooperation. If anyone has any more information or if you remember *anything* later, please contact us. We're counting on you to help us find whoever did this."

The crowd dispersed, leaving Ethan and Maria alone with the fallen horses whose blood soaked into the earth, marking the land with a dark stain of violence. The wind rustled through the trees, carrying a scent of gunpowder.

Ethan looked at Maria as she brushed the dirt from her knees, her expression resolute. "I'll check out that parking spot," she said. "See if they left anything behind."

He shook his head, a slight grin appearing on his face. "Just be careful, alright? Don't need to lose you out there in the dark."

She shot him a look. "I'll be fine, Wagner. I've been doing this awhile, remember?"

"I know, I know." He raised his hands in a mock surrender. "Just…be careful and keep your radio on."

As Ethan's gaze rested upon the fallen animals, a sound pierced the silence—a low, mournful howl—deep and haunting. It was the call of a lone wolf slicing through the air. Their attention shifted towards the hills, where faint silver moonlight traced the rugged edges.

Their eyes met. There were no words to be said.

II: The Path Ahead

JOHNATHAN CROW SWUNG OPEN the wooden door to Molly Butler's. He stepped into the glow of the lobby, where a soft, amber light spilled across the weathered wooden walls etched with the names of local residents. The rich aroma of fresh prime rib greeted his nostrils.

Peering through the large glass window, Jonathan watched the Arizona night settle over the small village of Greer, dusk pulling its shadowy curtain across the valley. Stepping inside this century-old lodge felt like a journey back in time - an echo of a simpler era.

He slipped off his hat, ran a hand over his hair, and settled at a high-top table in the bar. Though softened by age, his broad shoulders still carried the weight of countless years. He looked like the mountains he had spent his life protecting— strong and dependable but slowly giving way to time. A week's worth of stubble covered his face, more out of neglect than intention. He rubbed at it absent-mindedly, telling himself he was letting his beard grow out, though he knew it was only an excuse.

The bartender brought a cup of black coffee, placing it beside him with a grin. "Well, look what the wind blew down from the mountain," she said with a playful wink. They exchanged smiles as he wrapped his hands around the warm mug, savoring its heat. He took a slow sip, the bitterness anchoring him in the moment.

As his gaze drifted to the scene outside, it evoked memories of him and Marianne strolling along the Little Colorado River, picking wildflowers to brighten the cabin. Memories kept surfacing - her laughter echoing through the trees as she teased him about stomping down the trail, growling and swiping at branches like Bigfoot warding off tourists.

They had spent countless hours in nature together, sharing quiet moments and dreams of growing old together. Their love had been as enduring and steadfast as the mountains that embraced this beautiful valley. She was his constant, his anchor - and now, even two years later, he still missed her.

He also felt weary, not just from the loss of his wife but from the recent rescue of the Mexican grizzly bear, which had drawn him back into the familiar rhythm of work and duty. Before retiring as a game warden, the long hours had worn him down, but this was a different kind of fatigue. It wasn't just physical; it was emotional, too. Though he enjoyed teaching at Northland Pioneer College and giving summer lectures at the Butterfly Lodge Museum, he yearned for another adventure.

Suddenly, the bar patrons erupted in celebration when the Steelers scored a touchdown, the bartender twirling a Terrible Towel above her head like a cheer coach rallying the crowd. The crackle of logs in the fireplace echoed from the lobby, and the energy of the celebration around him felt unexpectedly uplifting.

A stranger gave him a high five, and his hand fell back onto the table made from a pine slab, where the knots and grain flowed like a natural piece of art. As he glanced at his hand, he noticed the lines etched into his skin – like a topographic map – seamlessly blending with the rugged patterns of the wood, as if both were threads woven into the fabric of these mountains.

Marianne's voice resonated in his mind, *"There's so much music left inside you, Jon."* That voice, gentle yet commanding, instilled strength in him as if she were sitting right there. At that moment, he no longer felt the need for answers.

He stood up and reached for his wallet to pay for his coffee. As he pushed his chair back into place, his eyes wandered behind the bar, landing on the mason jar labeled "Crow." He frowned; it was empty. "I need to sell more books," he mumbled.

Shaking his head, he turned left and spotted none other than Ethan Wagner making funny faces at him from across the bar. Opposite him, Maria Black tossed her head to the right, her hair flowing in the opposite direction and a smile that brightened the entire room.

Had they been…No.

He caught himself before the thought could fully materialize. Surely, they hadn't seen him before he stood up.

As Jonathan approached the table where Ethan and Maria were seated, he felt a sense of amusement. Their faces brightened when he sat down, but Ethan maintained his exaggerated facial expression, his eyes locked onto Jonathan with comical intensity.

"Didn't your mother warn you that your face could get stuck like that?" Johnathan said.

Before Ethan could respond, Maria grinned while leaning back in her chair. "Honestly, it would be an improvement."

"Oh, that really hurts, Maria," Ethan muttered, his smile lingering, never quite fading.

"Are you utterly devastated?" she smirked, arching her right eyebrow as he theatrically placed a hand over his heart.

"My heart just got a flat tire."

"God, you're dramatic," she chuckled.

Johnathan's eyes darted from Ethan to Maria and then to the way they locked eyes with each other. It had been a while since he'd seen them, and he realized how much he'd missed them.

"It's been too long," Jonathan said, prompting the two to turn their eyes back to him.

"Too long is right," Ethan said, leaning forward with his elbows on the table. "You've been hiding from us."

Maria shot him a look. "Give him a break, Officer Hotshot. He deserves some peace, especially from you!"

Jonathan gave a slight nod, his eyes lowering to the table. He wasn't sure how to articulate that the solitude he had been feeling hadn't exactly brought him peace. He pushed the thought aside, as men often do, and smiled.

"So," he said, looking up, "what's this about? Am I interrupting a date or a meeting?"

Maria's expression tightened with concern. Ethan quickly scanned the bar to ensure that no one was listening, then leaned in closer, his voice dropping to a whisper. "It's bad, Johnathan. Really bad."

Maria nodded, her eyebrows furrowed in a subtle frown. "Two wild horses were shot near Horseshoe Lake. Tourists were present and witnessed the entire event. Whoever did it wasn't shy about it either."

Jonathan frowned as he listened. He could picture the scene—the serene landscape shattered by gunfire, the horses falling, and all the tourists in horror. Just the thought of it made him feel nauseous.

"I don't understand people," he muttered. "Who would go after wild horses? They're no threat to anyone."

"That's what we're trying to figure out," Ethan said, his eyes sharp. "This wasn't random either. One of the witnesses claimed that the shooter's truck had been parked near Horseshoe Campground before the shooting."

Maria leaned forward, her voice steady. "They knew tourists from the valley would stop to admire the horses. They camped out, waited for people to arrive, and then shot them dead. I don't think this was some random act. It was statement."

"Christ Almighty." Jonathan shook his head, drumming his fingers on the table. He had seen a lot in his years, and he knew humans weren't exactly above being cruel, but the thought of someone targeting these animals in cold blood still made his chest ache. "Any leads?"

Ethan shook his head. "Nothing solid. They tried to see the license plate, but the truck sped off too quickly. We have a color and a broken taillight; that's about it. We cast the tire impressions at their campsite, so hopefully that will lead to something. But it will be tough to track them down until we obtain more information."

Jonathan's gaze drifted toward the garage door connecting the bar to the outdoor patio as he listened. Guests smiled, enjoying their dinner in the crisp evening air. Just beyond the lodge's safety lay a world where people like him knew all too well that sometimes these mountains concealed consequences.

Maria's voice brought him back. "It's not just about the horses, Jonathan. The way it's escalating. It's disturbing."

He met her gaze, a question in his eyes. "Escalating?"

She nodded; her face was tense. "It started with the horse shootings near Heber. Then we discovered traps on hiking trails, fires being started in areas where people don't typically recreate, and signs of something more sinister - hidden supply caches. These aren't just petty crimes, Jonathan. The frightening thing is that we don't know who they are or their endgame."

Ethan leaned back in his chair, folding his arms across his chest. "That's why we're here. We've been assigned to investigate, but this feels big, Jonathan. Like it could get messy, fast."

"Don't ask, Wagner." He said, clearly unamused.

Ethan's mouth quirked into a sad smile. "We could use you, Jonathan. You know these mountains like nobody else. And the people... they trust you."

Jonathan looked at Ethan, then at Maria. He could see the urgency in their eyes; however, the heaviness that came with those words wasn't something he could ignore. Assisting with another case wasn't that easy for him. At least not now. Not anymore.

Maria reached across the table, her hand resting on his arm. "We wouldn't ask if we didn't think it was necessary. You've already done so much. But... there's a lot at stake here. Who knows what they'll do next? Poison the Black River? I mean, the Apache Trout was just delisted - they're an ideal target for whatever political message these people are trying to send."

Jonathan's gaze drifted to her hand before returning to her face. He noticed the sincerity in her expression, the genuine belief that they could make a difference. And he wanted to embrace that belief as well.

"I don't know," he said at last. "After everything... it's been difficult to get back into it. People just make life difficult."

They sat silently for a moment, with a few cheers in the background as the football game continued. Jonathan recalled Marianne's voice in his head, reminding him that he still had *"a lot of music left inside him."*

Ethan's voice interrupted his train of thought. "Remember the grizzly? How we fought tooth and nail to keep it safe? We saved an entire species, Jonathan!"

Jonathan's jaw tightened as memories flooded back. The search for the grizzly had been one of the most thrilling experiences of his life, both spiritually and emotionally. After all, it was because of them the Mexican grizzly had returned to the White Mountains.

"Yeah, I remember," he said quietly.

Ethan's gaze softened. "That's why we need you. This is the same kind of threat, Jonathan. Only this time, we might be able to stop it before it spirals out of control."

"What's the plan?" Johnathan asked.

Maria exchanged a glance with Ethan. "We're planning to camp along the North Fork of the White River," she said. "Just below the Katie Hatch memorial. We thought it'd be a good starting point. We'll be able to hike upstream, look for clues, and see what we can find."

Her mention of the Katie Hatch memorial struck him more profoundly than he had anticipated. The memorial was for a brave seven-year-old girl who, in 1905, had wandered away from the family camp. Upon realizing she was missing, a search party was quickly assembled, assisted by Apache scouts. They found small footprints near Gomez Creek, but they soon disappeared. They focused their search only on the north side of the White River, assuming she would not dare to cross it. Weeks passed, and the effort to find her continued. Eventually, they extended their search to the south side of the river, and exactly twenty days after Katie's disappearance, the search concluded - nine miles from where it began. Her lifeless body was discovered.

Jonathan glanced back at them, his expression softening. "You always were the clever ones," he said with a hint of a smile.

Maria chuckled, though her gaze remained serious. "You've taught us well."

This was about safeguarding something sacred, something worth fighting for. He knew deep down that if he walked away now, he would regret it.

Ethan cleared his throat, breaking the silence. "So... you in?"

Jonathan glanced at them, his gaze lingering on each of their faces. They were younger and stronger, yet they bore the same weight he did and possessed the same understanding of what this work entailed. At that moment, he realized he couldn't let them go alone.

With a resigned sigh, he nodded. "Yeah, I'm in. But *only* as a consultant. Don't expect me to be lugging around rucksacks and flying around in helicopters!"

A smile spread across Ethan's face, and Maria's eyes brightened with relief. Jonathan glanced back at the table where he had enjoyed his coffee, and for a moment, he saw Marianne sitting there, smiling, her expression proud. He had made the right decision.

Ethan reached across the table and gave him a playful slap on the shoulder. "I knew you couldn't resist," he said, a hint of mischief in his eyes.

Jonathan let out a half-hearted chuckle, shaking his head. "You're going to owe me for this one, Wagner. I'm just a consultant!"

"Deal," Ethan replied, grinning.

Maria lifted her glass of water, her gaze full of warmth. "To old friends and new adventures."

They clinked glasses, which felt like a promise - a silent agreement to face whatever lay ahead, protect what they could, and fight for what mattered.

Ethan's expression turned serious again as they placed their glasses down. "There's something else you should know."

Jonathan raised an eyebrow, sensing the shift in tone. "What's that?"

Ethan looked at Maria before speaking. "The Chief's health. He's been struggling."

This struck Jonathan like a punch to the gut. Chief Grey Cloud was more than just a leader of the Apache tribe; he was a guide, a source of wisdom and strength for all who knew him. He resembled the soil, steady and unwavering, holding the land and its people together.

"Is it…?" Jonathan paused, uncertain about which word to choose. "Terminal?"

Maria nodded, her expression somber. "He doesn't want anyone to know, but… yes, it's serious. He's been pushing himself too hard."

Jonathan felt a tinge of guilt as he recalled the times he'd relied on the Chief for guidance and advice. He had taken it for granted as if the Chief would always be there. The thought of him struggling seemed unfathomable, like an elder forgetting the sacred songs of his people.

"He wants to join us for part of the investigation," Ethan said. "He's still connected to the land in ways we can never appreciate. If he can hold up, maybe he can help us find some answers."

Upon hearing about the Chief's declining health, Jonathan recognized that this was more than just another case; it felt personal for all of them.

"I'll be there," he said, his voice steady. "Whatever happens, we'll get to the bottom of this."

Ethan gave him a grateful look, and Maria squeezed his hand.

As they stood to leave, Ethan gently put his hand on his shoulder. "Just like old times, huh?"

Jonathan chuckled, a glimmer of the old fire igniting in his eyes. "Yeah, just like the good old days."

As they exited the lodge's front door, a wolf's howl pierced the dark silence, rising and falling in a haunting note that echoed across the valley. Ethan's gaze locked with Jonathan's while Maria's eyes flickered between them.

Silence fell.

III: Campfire Revelations

THE TRIO ADJUSTED THEIR PLANS and agreed to meet near the first bridge on Hawley Lake Road the following day. Jonathan arrived first, scanning the riverbank as if the water held answers to his questions. Maria followed shortly, lugging her 'mobile lab,' and fifteen minutes later, Ethan pulled up, hopping out of his truck with an energetic stride.

"Morning," Ethan said, adjusting his utility belt. "Hope you two got some rest. Gonna be a long day."

"Rest? What's that?" Maria replied with a smirk as she set up her equipment on the back of her Jeep. She opened the case, revealing a collection of tools and instruments that appeared out of place in the wilderness but were essential to their task.

Jonathan gave a small grunt of acknowledgment. "Long days aren't new to me. Let's get to work!"

Ethan leaned against the hood of his truck, flipping through his notepad. "I've been following up on leads from the horse shootings. It feels like chasing a ghost. Whenever we think we've found something, it vanishes."

He glanced at Maria, who was already elbow-deep in her analysis. "What about you? Find anything on those bullets?"

Maria didn't look up as she worked. "They're not standard rounds, that's for sure." She held up a small fragment, pinched between tweezers, and tilted it toward the light. "Tracer rounds. They track the flight of a bullet. Hunters don't typically use them—they are too expensive and reveal your position."

Jonathan crossed his arms, his brow furrowing. "So, what you're saying is we're not dealing with amateurs."

Maria nodded. "It's more sophisticated than I expected. Whoever's behind this either has military training or access to high-grade ammunition."

Ethan let out a low whistle. "I've got a bad feeling about this."

He straightened up and flipped to another page in his notebook. "I spent yesterday following up on tips from the hotline and talked to a few ranchers who had been in the area. Most of them were cooperative, but some tension was brewing. You know how it is—conservationists pushing for more restrictions and ranchers pushing back. Add wild horses to the mix, and things get heated."

"Any names?" Jonathan inquired, his tone sharp.

Ethan shook his head. "Nothing. One rancher mentioned seeing an old, rusted blue truck but couldn't give me much else. The plate number is still a mystery."

Maria glanced up from her work, a thoughtful expression on her face. "If they're using tracer rounds, there may be a way to track them. The pyrotechnic charge leaves a residue. If I can isolate it, we could narrow down where they acquired the ammunition."

Jonathan nodded. "Good. Let's hope it gives us something solid."

Maria worked meticulously, her gloved hands steady as she examined the fragment under a portable microscope in her small but efficient lab. She adjusted the lens until the surface details were in sharp focus.

"There," she murmured, pointing to a faint discoloration on the metal. "Do you see that? That's the residue from the pyrotechnic charge. Similar to fingerprints, tracer rounds leave a distinctive signature."

Ethan leaned over, squinting. "Okay, and that tells us what?"

Maria straightened up and pulled out a small reference guide. "If I cross-reference the chemical composition, I might be able to trace the manufacturer. It's not a guarantee, but it's a start."

Jonathan watched her work, and his respect for her continued to grow. "You've got quite a knack for this, Maria."

She flashed him a quick smile. "Dr. Hutlsch, my now-retired mentor, was a forensic expert. He ensured we practiced forensics because he believed it would be useful someday."

"Well, he clearly understood his subject," Ethan said with a chuckle, though his expression quickly turned serious again. "So, are you suggesting they might have acquired these rounds legally instead of through the black market?"

"Or stole them," Maria replied.

Jonathan's gaze shifted toward the river, his mind working through the implications.

The three spent the rest of the day working independently to advance the case. Ethan continued interviewing locals, circling back to anyone who might have seen the truck or heard gunshots. His frustration was evident as each lead turned into a dead end. The locals remained tight-lipped, either out of fear or loyalty to whoever might be responsible for the shootings.

Maria remained with her equipment, conducting tests and making notes. She identified more chemical markers and a scratch on the fragment, but each discovery raised further questions.

Following a previous lead, Jonathan hiked the trail where the woman had seen the parked truck. He climbed the ridge overlooking No Name Creek but found nothing except a few scattered pieces of litter.

By late afternoon, they regrouped, frustration evident on their faces. Ethan dropped onto a fallen tree, brushing dirt from his jacket sleeve. "Feels like we're going in circles," he muttered.

Maria sat beside him, closing her notebook. "We aren't. We have pieces of the puzzle; we just need to determine how they fit."

Jonathan stood a few feet away, his gaze fixed on the horizon. The sun began to dip, casting shadows across the landscape. He took a deep breath, inhaling the scent of pine and damp earth. "We'll get there," he said, his voice steady. "These things take time."

Ethan looked up at him, a hint of a smile pulling at his lips. "You always had the patience of a saint."

Jonathan turned, his expression softening. "I'm not a saint, Wagner. I'm just someone who has been around long enough to know that the truth doesn't come easily."

As the light faded, a pulsating beep from Maria's equipment pierced the silence, immediately drawing their attention. They gathered around her lab as she leaned over the screen, her eyes squinting in concentration as she examined the results.

"What is it?" Ethan asked.

Maria didn't respond immediately, her fingers flying across the keyboard. Then she looked up, her expression a blend of triumph and concern. "The tracer rounds—they're military-grade. Specifically designed for use in training exercises."

Ethan cursed under his breath. "Well, this just got a lot more complicated."

Maria nodded thoughtfully. "Whoever is behind this isn't just an average Joe. These are sophisticated individuals. They knew the investigators would piece this together - they're clearly sending a message."

Jonathan's jaw tightened. "Then we'd better figure out what it is before they send another one."

The mood was heavy yet determined as they packed up for the day. The puzzle pieces were beginning to come together, but the image they formed was concerning. The stakes were higher than any of them had anticipated, and the path ahead promised to be anything but simple.

Ethan's voice remained steady as he said, "Let's meet tomorrow at 5 pm." Maria offered him a small smile, her confidence intact.

Johnathan shook his head. "I'm meeting with a few people in Springerville tomorrow – there's talk of another wind farm being built off Highway 60. I'm not sure I'll make it."

Ethan scrunched his nose. "A wind farm? Great, just what we need – giant fans to cool off the cows!" he chuckled.

The following day, the Rendezvous Diner was unusually quiet, with the steady drip of the coffee machine cutting through the soft murmur of a few scattered patrons. Maria sat in the corner, sipping warm tea and jotting notes, her mind focused on bullet fragments and tracer rounds. Nearby, two ranchers leaned in, their conversation catching her attention.

"I'm tellin' you, it's them outsiders stirrin' up trouble," the older of the two muttered, his hand tightening around his mug. "First the fires, now the horses? It don't sit right."

The younger man nodded, his voice low but bitter. "Heard there was a fight over in Alpine last night. At the bar. Couple of strangers, mouthy types. Bet they have somethin' to do with all of this."

Maria's pen paused. Pretending to adjust her notebook, she listened to the ranchers' words: outsiders, fights, fires. The pieces fit with a rusted blue truck, expensive ammo, and whispers of people causing trouble. This was bigger than just a few disgruntled locals; it was deliberate.

She didn't waste another second. Tossing a few dollars onto the table for her tea, she hurried out into the crisp morning air, her mind racing ahead of Ethan's reaction and the weight of what she needed to tell him.

By late afternoon, Ethan and Maria had established their camp at the confluence of Paradise Creek and the North Fork of the White River. Towering pines enveloped them, providing a sense of seclusion. Ethan crouched by the fire, encouraging the kindling to ignite, while Maria unpacked her equipment with careful attention.

Ethan tossed a few larger logs onto the crackling flames. "You seem awfully intense."

She paused, meeting his gaze with a raised eyebrow. "You've known me how long?"

He beamed, stretching out his arms. "Fair point," he said, then gently kissed her on the cheek.

Ethan settled into a chair, stretching his legs before he spoke. "So," he said after a moment, "How was the Rendezvous? Was there a line to get in?"

Maria hesitated, gripping her notebook tighter before she sat across from him. "The locals are on edge. They're pointing fingers at outsiders - apparently, there was a fight at the bar in Alpine last night. Word is, out-of-towners are causing trouble."

Ethan frowned. "Fights in Alpine usually don't create waves. What's different this time?"

"They mentioned the fires and the dead horses. It's all starting to feel connected now." She leaned forward, the flames reflecting in her eyes. "What if this is some sort of organized group that isn't even from the mountain?"

"Like someone trying to take down the big guy?" Ethan sighed. "What's going to be accomplished by killing horses and destroying the environment?"

They sat in silence.

"Do you ever get tired of this?" Ethan asked suddenly, his tone light, almost teasing. "Always fighting against people who don't respect the land and its wildlife."

"You mean, do I ever want a normal nine-to-five?" Maria smirked. "Not a chance."

"Figured," he said with a grin. "But you gotta admit, a little boredom wouldn't hurt now and then."

Snap!

The unmistakable sound of a twig snapping underfoot interrupted their conversation. Both Ethan and Maria froze. Ethan instinctively reached for the flashlight on his belt while Maria picked hers up from the ground. They turned them on at the same time, the beams of light slicing through the darkness like a blade.

"Who's there?" Ethan called.

The forest stood still; the only sound was the rustling of leaves in the breeze. Then, a figure emerged from the shadows at the edge of the tree line: it was Jonathan Crow.

"Well, you're a long way from Greer, old man." Ethan joked.

Jonathan stopped, his hands casually resting at his sides. "I thought I'd do some tracking," he said, his tone neutral and almost disinterested.

Ethan crossed his arms; his skepticism was evident. "Tracking?"

Jonathan shrugged and stepped closer, allowing the campfire to illuminate his face. His beard appeared a bit thicker, and his eyes looked tired but sharp. "Just looking for signs," he stated. "Didn't expect to stumble upon your camp."

Maria narrowed her eyes. "Oh, really?"

Jonathan met her gaze steadily, the corner of his mouth twitching in what could be mistaken for a smile. "You two aren't exactly hard to find out here. Flashlights blazing and voices carrying across Horseshoe Lake - you're like a pair of neon signs in the woods."

Ethan snorted, pulled out another chair, and motioned for Jonathan to sit. "Fine. Join the party."

Jonathan purposefully lowered himself into the chair, exuding a quiet strength that radiated even in the smallest actions.

"What are you *really* doing here, Jonathan?" Maria asked after a moment.

He didn't answer right away, gazing into the fire as if he were searching for the right words. "You asked me to help," he finally said, his tone low. "I suppose I'm trying to figure out if I still can."

Ethan's expression softened, but he tried to conceal it with his usual humor. "Well, you're off to a great start. Sneaking up on us like the Mogollon Monster."

Jonathan chuckled, the sound dry but genuine. "Old habits."

Maria leaned forward, resting her elbows on her knees. "If you're here, this isn't exactly standard consulting work. So, what has changed?"

"Nothing changed. I found some tracks near Horseshoe Lake and, uh, this," Jonathan said, looking at Ethan as he pulled something out of his pocket. It was a piece of green and khaki camouflage fabric. He then turned to Maria, "I heard about the fight," as he handed the fabric to Ethan.

Maria nodded, repeating what she had told Ethan, "People are talking about outsiders."

He nodded while glancing at Ethan. "This fabric is light and durable, but it's not military standard. There's too much polyester."

"What's that?" Maria pointed at a rusty brown stain on the back.

Ethan eyed it cautiously. "It could be dried blood. Maybe you can run a scan on it to find out?"

Maria paused for a moment, considering, before reaching into her bag and pulling out a plastic bag. She took the material from Ethan and carefully sealed it inside.

"I will run it first thing tomorrow morning. It is fairly dry, but I might be able to add some moisture and lift something from the threads. The scanners I use for identifying animal samples should assist in determining whether it is human or not."

"If the sample is human, we can try to match it with any of our databases and see if we get a response," Ethan mumbled. "We might be able to obtain a name and cross-reference it with the truck."

"The woods have a way of keeping secrets," Johnathan said quietly. "But they also have a way of revealing them if you know where to look."

His words lingered in the air, punctuated by the soft crackle of the fire. The forest around them felt alive, with rustling leaves and the haunting calls of elk bugling in the rut serving as a constant reminder that they weren't alone.

"Do you ever think about what comes next?" Maria asked, her voice soft.

Ethan shrugged. "Next is whatever's in front of us. That's the job."

Jonathan nodded slightly, his eyes fixed on the fire. "The job is never really done," he said quietly. "Out here, it's not just work; it's who we are. It defines us."

Maria gazed at him, her expression enigmatic. "That's why you returned."

Jonathan didn't respond immediately, his hands tightening briefly on the arms of his chair. "Maybe I don't know how to stay away," he admitted. "Or maybe it's because I can't leave everything in the hands of you two knuckleheads!"

Ethan chuckled. "Oh, so you're a babysitter now."

"I suppose," Johnathan muttered, "I guess I'm still trying to come to terms with everything. Like the grizzly." He hummed, thinking of Marianne and how much he wished she were with him. "It takes its toll. It gives you just enough sense of invincibility to keep you moving, but then you find yourself in a place you can't escape."

Ethan nodded absentmindedly while Maria's gaze rested on the fire.

"But the pain of never trying… that's a burden no one can escape."

IV: The Land Never Lies

THE FOREST WAS STILL, its pre-dawn quiet broken only by the occasional rustle of underbrush and the distant howl of a few coyotes. Ethan stirred, sitting up in his sleeping bag and rubbing the back of his neck. The faint glow of the campfire embers illuminated the outside of the tent.

Maria was already awake, crouched by the fire pit, coaxing a small flame back to life. Jonathan sat on a log nearby, his wide-brimmed hat pulled low over his face; however, it was clear from his posture that he wasn't asleep. The air carried a biting chill, reminding everyone that the sun had yet to rise fully.

Then, the sound came—hoofbeats.

They were faint at first, a rhythmic pounding that seemed to emanate from nowhere. Ethan froze, his eyes darting toward the tree line. Maria stood. Jonathan lifted his head, his body tense yet composed.

"You hear that?" Ethan whispered.

"Yeah," Maria replied, her voice low.

Jonathan remained silent. He stood up slowly, his movements deliberate as he reached for his pepper spray. Ethan mirrored him, clutching his firearm while exchanging a glance with Maria.

The hoofbeats grew louder, echoing off the trees like a heartbeat. The trio stood shoulder to shoulder, their eyes fixed on the sound. The daylight was dim, and shadows lifted around them, revealing nothing but trees and swirling fog.

Then, the rider emerged.

Chief Grey Cloud sat atop a powerful black horse, its coat glistening faintly in the dim light. The Chief's figure was commanding yet frail—a stark contrast that rendered the scene almost surreal. His shoulders were slightly hunched, his breath labored, and his hands trembled as he held the reins. Still, his presence bore a weight that silenced the surrounding forest.

"Chief?" Ethan called out, holstering his firearm. "What are you doing out here?"

Chief Grey Cloud didn't respond immediately. He gently urged his horse closer, the animal moving with effortless grace despite the obvious frailty of its rider. As the Chief approached the campfire, his face became visible - etched with deep lines, each marking the passage of years spent battling time, nature, and forces threatening their way of life.

Jonathan stepped forward, his voice calm but concerned. "Chief, you shouldn't be out here. You should be taking care of yourself."

The Chief dismounted slowly, his movements deliberate yet resolute. His feet struck the ground with surprising firmness despite the unsteadiness of his legs. He paused momentarily, steadying himself against the horse before speaking, while Jonathan tied the horse to a tree.

"The land called me here," he said, his voice raspy but strong. "I could not ignore it. The spirits are restless; the souls, they yearn to be free from tragedy."

Maria exchanged a glance with Ethan, her brow furrowed. "The land called to you?" she asked cautiously.

Chief Grey Cloud's gaze locked with hers, piercing and clear despite the fatigue in his body. He coughed before speaking, his voice raspy yet unwavering. "The signs are present. The imbalance intensifies. The forest senses it. The animals perceive it."

His words hung in the air, heavy with meaning. "What kind of imbalance are we talking about?" Ethan asked.

The Chief turned to him, his gaze steady. "Nature is a delicate thing, Ethan. When one thread is pulled, the entire weave is at risk. You've seen it yourselves—the fires, the horses, the whispers of men who do not belong to this land."

Jonathan's jaw tightened. "And what do you think?"

The Chief nodded. "The earth speaks of change, of danger. Those who seek to control it will only bring chaos."

Maria stepped closer, her voice softer now. "But who are they? The ones behind this? The data suggests militants; the people are talking about outsiders."

"Titles do not matter." The Chief's eyes flicked to her, then back to the fire. "They are merely those who have lost respect for the land. Those who view it only as something to conquer, to take from. They are not new, but their presence grows bolder."

Jonathan's gaze fell to the ground, his thoughts becoming introspective. He had spent his entire life fighting to safeguard these mountains, yet the battles appeared relentless. The weight of the Chief's words bore down on him heavily.

"Why are you here, Chief?" Jonathan asked, concerned about his health. "I mean, there's a hell of a lot of people out there who don't respect the land, but they don't go shooting horses and starting fires because of it."

The Chief stepped forward, placing a hand on Jonathan's shoulder. "Because of you," he said, pointing to the heart in his chest. "Because you still understand what it means to protect, not to possess. This fight is not just yours—it is ours, for all beneath the flesh is interconnected through the land. To the root and the rock that support our homes and embrace our graves."

These words fell upon him, and for a moment, Johnathan was silent. He felt the others' gazes upon him, waiting, but his attention was on the Chief.

They sat around the campfire as the first light of dawn touched the surrounding mountains, the fire burning low yet steady. The Chief spoke again, his voice carrying a quieter weight now. He told them of dreams, of visions he couldn't quite explain but couldn't ignore. He spoke of wolves and fire, shadows moving through the trees, and the feeling that something old and dangerous was stirring.

Maria listened intently, her scientific mind attempting to piece together the symbolism in his words. Conversely, Ethan leaned back slightly, his expression thoughtful yet guarded.

Jonathan said little, his gaze fixed on the horizon as the sunlight glimmered off Paradise Creek.

Ethan broke the silence first. "So, what's the plan?" he asked, looking at the others. "Because I'm all for listening to the land, but we have real people involved in this. Dangerous ones."

Maria nodded. "He's right. We can't ignore the practical side of this. If a whole group is involved, we need to figure this out before it escalates. God knows what'll happen if they start targeting establishments in town or start putting people in danger."

Jonathan finally looked away from the horizon; his expression was resolute. "We follow the signs," he said. "The land has never lied to us before."

Ethan raised an eyebrow but didn't argue. Instead, he stood, brushing off his jeans. "Well, I think we need help. I'll radio in and see if we can get more eyes out here."

Maria smiled faintly and stood up. "I will continue working on the evidence."

Chief Grey Cloud then said, "I nearly forgot." He handed Ethan a piece of leather.

Ethan furrowed his brow, confusion crossing his face. "What's this? Just some letters and numbers carved into leather."

The Chief nodded. "On my way here, I spotted a blue truck by the ditch camp. I thought you might want the license plate. Sorry, I don't own a pen, so I had to use my fingernail."

V: An Ancient Oak

MARIA CROUCHED BESIDE HER GEAR, her fingers rifling through an assortment of supplies in search of a small camp kettle. The morning air was still cool, and the quiet was broken only by the soft rustling of leaves and the occasional song of a northern flicker. Nearby, Jonathan stood, his movements slow yet purposeful as he stretched his back. With a grimace, he arched backward, which cracked loudly with a series of pops.

"Getting old, Crow?" Maria teased, not looking up as she added another log to the fire. "Or is that just your spine trying to escape your body?"

Jonathan chuckled as he reached for his boots. "I've just got more miles on me than a truck without shocks."

Sitting at his notebook and struggling to keep his eyes open, Ethan jokingly said, "Hey, could you two keep it down? Some of us are trying to solve a mystery, not start a circus."

"Well, we were up well before you and started working," Maria replied, smirking as she set the camp kettle over the fire. "You know, like adults."

Jonathan chuckled, shaking his head as he laced up his boots. "If you're calling yourself an adult, I've got bad news for you."

Ethan shook his head, running a hand through his hair, causing it to stand up as if he had just placed his finger in an electrical socket.

Maria glanced over at Chief Grey Cloud, who was sitting on an old tree stump about thirty yards away from the camp. His head was lowered, and his eyes were closed, but it was clear that he was not asleep. She couldn't help but wonder what it must be like to have such a deep, ancient connection to the land, to perceive what others couldn't, to hear frequencies most people overlooked, and to grasp certain truths about the universe that remained hidden from most.

Johnathan noticed how her eyes lingered on the Chief and let out a low hum as he reached to pour himself a cup of black coffee. "He's been like that as long as I've known him," he said, placing the kettle back onto the fire. "He likes to sit in silence and listen, not with his ears but with his soul. These mountains somehow speak to him, whispering secrets and revealing truths that go way beyond my understanding."

Ethan stretched his arms above his head, yawning loudly. "Yeah, well, these mountains better be saying something useful today. We need all the help we can get."

Maria shot him a look, but her expression softened as Jonathan sat by the fire, coffee cup in hand. "You've got stories, don't you?" she asked, her tone now lighter. "You and the Chief go way back."

Jonathan smiled faintly, picked up a twig, and drew a circle in the dirt between his legs. "Oh, plenty of stories. Did I ever tell you he tried to kick me out of his forest when we first met?"

Ethan set his notebook down and raised an eyebrow. "Seriously? How did that go?"

Jonathan stirred his coffee with his finger, a smirk playing on his lips. "Not well. I was tracking a mountain lion that had come too close to Buffalo Crossing Campground. Chief confronted me near the confluence of the Black River, told me to leave, and said I was trampling all over sacred ground."

Maria leaned forward, her eyes filled with curiosity. "What did you do?"

"I apologized," Jonathan said with a shrug. "Then I asked him for help."

"And?" Ethan prompted.

Jonathan's smile grew broader. "He complained the entire time, but ultimately, he found that cat better than I ever could."

Ethan laughed. "That sounds about right. The Chief certainly has a way of making you feel as though you're the one slowing him down."

The trio shared a laugh, and for a moment, Ethan could have sworn he saw the Chief smile. The fire continued to crackle, its warmth blending with the crisp morning air while the scent of fresh coffee lingered.

And then came the sound that brought nothing but misery.

Gunshots.

Three sharp cracks, distant yet unmistakable, shattered the morning's tranquility. Ethan's head snapped toward the forest, his expression instantly serious. "That came from Horseshoe Lake," he said, his voice low and urgent.

Maria froze, her hand halfway to the coffee pot. "Are you sure?"

"Positive," Ethan said, already reaching for his boots and utility belt. "I know sounds echo out here, but that was definitely the direction."

Jonathan stood, his hand instinctively reaching for the can of pepper spray clipped to his belt. His expression changed from relaxed to grim. "We need to move. Now."

The Chief sighed, attempting to stand, but a cough suddenly shook his weakened frame. Maria noticed immediately, her concern deepening. Gently yet respectfully, she urged him to remain at camp. "It wouldn't be wise for you to push yourself," she said. "You can barely catch your breath. Rest here, and we'll be back."

"It is my duty; I must…" he muttered, coughing into a white cloth and wincing as he noticed dark red blood spreading across it.

"It's your duty, Chief. But right now, you need to rest." Jonathan shook his head as the Chief stubbornly protested. "The forest needs you, but it needs you alive and well."

The Chief exhaled deeply and gave a slight, rigid nod before settling back onto the tree stump.

Maria nodded as she quickly packed her gear into her bag. "If it's poachers, we might still have a chance to catch them."

Ethan slung his rucksack over his shoulder, his movements swift yet controlled. "Can we leave him?"

Jonathan didn't answer, his gaze fixed towards the sound of the gunshots. The unspoken consequences lingered between them as they moved out, their boots crunching on the forest floor while they hiked up the canyon alongside Horseshoe Creek to reach the lake.

The vast meadow separating Highway 260 from Horseshoe Lake lay quiet, with Green's Peak looming in the background. The trio slowed as they hiked around the dam and into the clearing, their breathing still heavy from the hurried trek. Near the meadow, the lake shimmered, its calm surface belying the tension that weighed down the air.

Then they saw it.

A horse lay crumpled, its legs sprawled awkwardly as if it had collapsed mid-gait. A dark pool of blood had spread beneath its body; the red liquid against the yellowed autumn grass was a sickening sight. The hum of flies, like miniature drones, surrounded the carcass.

Maria approached first, her hand instinctively covering her mouth and nose against the salty, rusty scent of blood that filled the air. The smell was thick, a pungent mix of disturbed soil and the faint, sickly scent of decaying flesh. She stopped a few feet away, crouching as her eyes carefully surveyed the scene.

The horse's chest had been torn open, the wound jagged and raw. Blood dripped from the torn edges of its hide, thick and glistening under the sunlight. The shot was precise, a clean entry at the level of the heart, but its aftermath was devastating. The bullet had splintered bone as it tore through, leaving a gaping exit wound. Shattered ribs jutted outward, their sharp edges piercing through its mangled flesh.

Maria's voice was steady, though taut with tension. "Same caliber as before. Whoever did this wanted this horse dead - with one shot."

Jonathan stood a few steps back, his jaw clenched tightly. The horse had struggled, leaving its tracks in a confused pattern leading to its final resting place. Beyond the carcass, the flattened grass gave way to scuff marks, suggesting the presence of tire tracks.

Ethan stepped closer, his boots sinking into the blood-soaked ground. He crouched beside the dead horse, his expression grim as he examined the body. "This wasn't just a kill," he said quietly. "Look at the flank. They carved something."

Maria leaned in, her stomach twisting as her gaze fell upon the carving. Someone had slashed into the horse's hide, leaving behind three crude, jagged letters.

Jonathan's voice was low, nearly a growl. "What does R.A.I. mean?"

Ethan swore under his breath, rising quickly and stepping back. "It stands for 'Resist All Influence.'"

Maria frowned, "Resist all influence? What is this, some kind of anti-government group?" Her tone was filled with both curiosity and unease.

Jonathan knelt, his face inches from the ground as he studied the tire tracks leading away from the clearing. His hand hovered over the faint impressions of the tracks, fingers brushing the dirt. "They were definitely in a hurry," he said, his voice steady despite the scene before him. "If they're leaving messages like this, they're not just making a statement – they're declaring war."

Ethan nodded, his jaw tightening. "Nah, this isn't a war. They're just trying to intimidate us." He motioned toward the tire tracks, his frustration boiling over. "If I had to guess, I'd say it was the same truck. It's probably the one that the Chief saw."

Maria stood, brushing her hands against her jeans as if trying to rid herself of the horror she had just witnessed. "Then we need to figure out who they're trying to intimidate and why. Because if this keeps happening…" She trailed off, her words hanging ominously in the still air.

Jonathan stood slowly, his eyes fixed on the mutilated horse. His expression remained passive, but the tension in his clenched fists revealed the anger simmering beneath the surface. "Ethan, run that license plate the Chief gave you. Maria, call BLM to arrange a pickup – we need to get this poor animal out of here."

The trio returned to camp later that afternoon. Before diving into the tasks related to the shooting, they planned to give the Chief a ride back to Whiteriver. However, upon their return, they discovered that the Chief was no longer there, though his horse was still hitched to the same tree. Ethan, noticing the campfire had died down, began poking at the embers with a stick, his knee bouncing with impatience. He glanced at his field watch, the sharp tick of the second hand pulling his focus as if it were a magnet.

Maria stood a few feet away, arms crossed, her eyes scanning the tree line. Her usual calm demeanor shifted, replaced by a tense posture. "He's been gone too long," she murmured, almost to herself.

Sitting on a log by the fire, Jonathan poured the last bit of coffee into his tin mug and swirled it around. He hadn't said much since their return. He set his mug down and looked at Maria. "He's been doing this routine for years, probably just lost track of time."

Maria shook her head. "Something feels off. He didn't seem well when we left. He was coughing up blood, Jonathan."

Ethan let out a deep breath, tossing the stick aside. "You're right. We need to go find him." He stood up and began packing his gear. "Jonathan, you know this terrain better than anyone. We'll follow you."

Jonathan nodded, rising slowly and stretching his legs. "Fair enough," he said, although his tone carried a heaviness that revealed his unease.

Maria pulled her phone from her pocket and held it out to Jonathan. "Here, use this. Call his son Bidzil. We might need more help if he's wandered too far."

Jonathan hesitated before grabbing the phone, his calloused fingers dwarfed by the slim device. He muttered about "damn technology" as he fumbled with it, then quickly dialed the number. Bidzil answered almost immediately, and Jonathan got straight to the point. "Chief's been gone too long. We're heading up the North Fork of the White River; you cover Paradise Creek."

When the call ended, Jonathan returned the phone to Maria without a word. "Let's move," he said, his voice low and steady.

The canyon swallowed them as they marched upstream. Shafts of sunlight broke through the dense canopy above, creating shifting patterns of gold on the damp earth below. Occasionally, the snap of a twig underfoot or the bugle of a distant elk reminded them that others shared the wilderness with them.

Maria walked beside Jonathan, her eyes continually scanning the trees for any sign of movement. "Do you think he's alright?" she asked, her voice just above a whisper.

Johnathan's face remained impassive, his eyes searching for any sign of the Chief. "He's tougher than he appears," he said, though the tension in his jaw revealed his concern. "But these mountains can be unforgiving, even for someone like him."

Ethan walked a few steps behind. "It feels too quiet out here," he murmured. "I don't like it."

They pressed on, their pace quickening as their unease deepened. The forest felt oppressive, the towering pines leaning in as if holding their breath. Jonathan was the first to notice it. At the base of an ancient oak tree, just off the river's edge and barely visible through the thick underbrush, something slumped against the tree. He stopped suddenly, raising his hand to signal the others to halt.

"There," he said, his voice rough.

Maria and Ethan followed his gesture, their eyes quickly locking onto the figure. The three of them moved forward in unison, their footsteps cautious yet swift. As they drew nearer, the details sharpened, and Ethan felt his breath catch in his throat.

Jonathan knelt beside him with care. The Chief's hands rested in his lap, palms facing up as if he was offering something unseen to the heavens. His skin appeared pale, and his features were drawn, yet a strange peace was present.

Maria stood frozen, her hand over her mouth as she tried to process what she saw. "No," she whispered. "No, no…"

Ethan crouched next to Jonathan, his expression stricken. "He's… is he…?"

Jonathan placed a gentle yet firm hand on the Chief's shoulder. "He's gone," he said softly.

None of them moved. The ancient oak appeared to cradle the Chief, its twisted roots enveloping him like protective arms. The late afternoon sun filtered through the leaves, casting dappled light over his still form and bestowing an almost sacred quality upon the scene.

Suddenly, a sound pierced the tense silence—a faint but deliberate rustling in the undergrowth. Maria's head snapped toward the noise, holding her breath and widening her eyes. There, just a few yards away and barely concealed in the shadow of a tree, stood a lone wolf, its eyes gleaming with intensity.

It was large, its fur a striking blend of gray and silver. Its icy blue eyes locked onto each of them, unblinking and unnervingly intelligent. There was no trace of aggression, only a calm presence that felt more like an observer than a predator.

"Ethan," Maria said softly, nudging him.

He followed her glance and froze. "What the hell…"

Jonathan turned slowly, his eyes directed toward the wolf. None of them spoke for a moment, their breath caught in their throats. The wolf's eyes shifted to the Chief, its expression—if it could even be called that—impossible to decipher. It stood perfectly still, staring intently at the Chief's body.

Maria broke the silence, her voice barely above a whisper. "It's not collared. That's... that's impossible. All alphas in this territory are tagged."

Jonathan didn't take his eyes off the animal. "Perhaps it isn't one of ours."

Ethan's hand twitched toward his belt, but Jonathan halted him with a sharp look. "Don't," he said firmly. "It's not here to harm us."

Then, the wolf's gaze shifted to Jonathan, and something extraordinary happened. One eye remained a deep, icy blue, while the other transformed into a warm amber color – the exact hue of the Chief's eyes. It held its ground for a moment longer, then slowly turned its head toward the forest as it slipped silently into the shadows.

Ethan blinked several times, his eyes now wide open. "Did... did everyone see what I just saw?" He glanced back at the spot where the wolf had stood. "The way its eye changed – am I losing my mind, or was that real?"

"It was real," Jonathan responded. He reached for his water bottle and pulled out a red handkerchief. Pouring water onto the fabric, he gently wiped the Chief's arms and hands.

"What are you doing?" Maria asked, her voice hesitant.

Jonathan didn't look up. "It's a cleansing ritual," he said. "For his journey home."

Maria hesitated, torn between her logical instincts and her deep respect for Jonathan and the Chief. "We need to call Bidzil," she said, pulling out her phone. But when she glanced at the screen, her frown deepened. "No signal."

Jonathan finished wiping the Chief's hands, then folded the handkerchief carefully and placed it on the ground beside him. "Then we will stay with the Chief until they find us," he said.

Ethan finally asked, "Do you think that wolf - ?"

"It wasn't a wolf," Jonathan interrupted, his tone calm but unwavering, leaving no room for doubt.

Maria glanced at him, her expression skeptical yet curious. "What do you mean?"

"It was the Chief," Jonathan said, his tone dark and unwavering.

As the sun dipped lower, it enveloped the forest in hues of yellow and orange, reminiscent of the fading embers of a fire that could never truly extinguish – one destined to be reborn once again.

VI: The Ceremony

BIDZIL AND FIVE OTHER APACHE MEN stood in a solemn circle around the Chief's body, their expressions stoic yet weighed down by grief. The air was filled with reverence, broken only by the soft rustle of wind through the trees and the distant chirping of evening crickets.

One of the men stepped forward, carrying an intricately carved wooden symbol. Kneeling beside the Chief, he placed the token carefully on his chest. Nearby, another man lit a bundle of dried sage, its fragrant smoke curling gently into the sky. The sharp, earthy aroma enveloped the air as if purifying the space around them.

Ethan and Maria stood several paces back out of respect, their postures rigid with discomfort. Ethan shifted his weight from one foot to the other, his hands shoved awkwardly into his pockets. Maria, ever analytical, observed the scene with quiet intensity, her brow furrowed in thought.

"What's the symbol for?" Ethan asked, his voice hushed but curious.

Standing just behind them, Jonathan kept his gaze fixed on the ceremony. His voice was low and calm. "It's a mark of protection, meant to guide and shield the spirit on its journey."

Before either could respond, the rhythmic beat of drums began – soft at first, then steadily growing louder with each strike. Two Apache men sat cross-legged beneath the tree, their hands striking the taut leather hide in perfect harmony with rhythmic precision.

Then, from the shadows of the trees, four crown dancers emerged.

Their towering headdresses swayed gently in the breeze, adorned with intricate patterns of feathers that glimmered in the fading light. Bold, sacred designs painted their faces, the vivid colors striking against their skin. With each step, the soft jingle of native bells echoed, unifying their movements.

Ethan straightened, his eyes darting among each figure. "What's happening now?" he asked, his voice laced with uncertainty.

Jonathan tilted his head, his voice low and steady. "It's a story," he explained. "The dance symbolizes the bond between the land, their ancestors, and the Chief. It honors him – a reminder that the living and the departed are always connected."

The drums thundered louder, their rhythm swelling as the dancers' movements became more mesmerizing. Their steps flowed like the pulse of nature itself—steady, then bursting into wild, chaotic energy, mirroring the cycles of life and death. A melodic chant rose above the drumming, their voices weaving together in a deep, resonant cry that filled the surrounding forest.

Maria unfolded her arms, her expression a blend of wonder and unease. "It's... beautiful," she murmured, her voice barely above a whisper.

Jonathan nodded, his eyes never leaving the dancers. "It is."

As the dance reached its peak, the dancers stepped back, their movements slowing until they stood still. Their headdresses cast ghostly shadows in the fading light. Without a word, they melted into the forest, their figures disappearing into the shadows as silently as they had appeared.

The drumming ceased, the final beat resonating like the last contraction of the heart.

Bidzil and the others knelt beside the Chief, lifting his body with care. The blanket covering him shimmered in the golden light, its beadwork catching the final rays of the sun. Together, they began their journey home.

As the group vanished into the distance, the first stars appeared, faint pinpricks of light against the darkening sky. Jonathan stood still, a tear lingering in his eye, refusing to fall as he gazed into the distance. Ethan and Maria remained beside him, their silence heavy with the weight of the Chief's loss.

"Do you think his spirit...?" Ethan asked, his voice unwavering.

"I do," Jonathan replied confidently. "His ancestors are with him now."

Above them, the ancient oak stood tall and silent, its branches reaching upward like arms lifting the Chief toward the heavens. As they turned away, the stars shone brighter, their light mingling with the promise of nightfall and the distant call of a wolf, urging them onward.

They made their way back to camp, now shrouded in darkness. Ethan absentmindedly poked at the fire's extinguished embers while Maria leaned against her pack, her gaze fixed on the deep, impenetrable blackness. Jonathan sat apart from them in the spot where the Chief had once been, lost in thought. The weight of their loss hung heavily in the air, unspoken but felt by all.

Then, a howl shattered the silence.

It sliced through the silence like a blade, long and mournful, rising from the depths of the wilderness and extending endlessly into the night. Ethan froze, his grip tightening on the stick he held. Maria stiffened, her eyes darting toward the tree line.

"That's really close," Ethan muttered, his voice barely audible.

Jonathan stood up suddenly, his expression fierce and resolute. "It's the call of the wolf," he stated.

Ethan looked at him, confused. "What do you mean?"

Jonathan nodded as he turned to grab his rucksack. "The Chief once told me a story about a spirit wolf – one that guides lost souls into the afterlife. He said the wolf's howl is a sign, a summons to those chosen to walk in its path. We're being called."

Maria furrowed her brow as she glanced between them. "You mean we're being called to follow the wolf?"

Jonathan didn't respond directly. Instead, he pulled out his flashlight and checked the beam to ensure the batteries were good. "I'm going," he said flatly. "You can stay here if you want."

"Are you going out there now?" Ethan asked, glancing at Maria for reassurance.

Jonathan shouldered his rucksack and moved toward the tree line, pausing to glance back at them. "That wasn't just any wolf," he said, his voice calm yet firm. "We all know that. You can stay or come along; it's up to you."

Ethan glanced at Maria, noticing the sharp look in her eyes that seemed to say, "Let's go." "You saw what I saw," she said, her voice steady. "He's right. That's no ordinary wolf." With that, she grabbed her bag and put on her headlamp.

Ethan groaned as he grabbed his gear. "Alright, alright," he muttered, tossing aside the stick he had been holding before jogging after them. "Because that's what sane people do – chase howls in the night," he grumbled.

As they ventured deeper into the dark forest, everything felt unnervingly alive. Each sound was amplified, and every sway of the trees was exaggerated by the beam of their flashlights. The bugling calls of elk echoed through the woods, while above them, an owl's call questioned their decision.

"Why does it always feel… creepy at night?" Ethan whispered, his voice tense.

Jonathan didn't answer, his flashlight moving methodically across the forest floor before sweeping up to scan the cliff. He moved with a confidence that contrasted with the unease in the air. Maria walked closely behind him, her expression a mix of skepticism and concern.

Suddenly, another howl pierced the air, much closer this time, sending a chill down their spines.

Jonathan froze, his heart pounding as he raised his flashlight toward a nearby ridge. The beam cut through the darkness, illuminating the jagged Malapais rock at the summit. There, standing like a dark sentinel, was the wolf.

Its silver coat shimmered softly in the light, but its eyes— one icy blue and the other a deep amber—held their attention. The wolf stood still, gazing down at them with an unsettling, eerie awareness.

Jonathan exhaled slowly. "It's him," he murmured, almost reverently.

Ethan stepped back, his eyes darting from the wolf to Jonathan. "You don't actually believe—"

"Look at its eyes," Jonathan interrupted, his voice tense. "Tell me that's not the Chief."

Ethan stared up at the wolf, swallowing hard. "So... we're actually following it, right? That's the plan?"

Maria nodded slowly, her eyes fixed on the wolf. "I believe it," she said softly. "There's no other explanation for what we saw."

Jonathan moved purposefully toward the ridge where the wolf stood, leaving Ethan and Maria no choice but to follow.

The climb was steep and treacherous, with loose rocks shifting dangerously beneath their feet. Jonathan moved steadily, using his flashlight to search for the safest footholds. Maria struggled to keep up, her breaths quickening as the incline grew steeper. Halfway up, her foot slipped, causing her to gasp and tumble to her knees with a sharp cry.

"Got you!" Ethan said, grabbing her arm just in time to prevent her from sliding off the cliff. "Careful, Maria."

She nodded, her face pale as she steadied herself. "Thanks; I'm okay," she said, regaining her footing.

Jonathan paused and turned back to look at them. "Stay close," he said, his tone firm yet gentle.

They could no longer see the wolf but followed its tracks toward Paradise Creek. As they descended, the beam of Jonathan's flashlight fell on something unusual – a faded turquoise generator, its metal rusted with age, standing beside a decaying wooden structure.

As they passed the old structure, strange signs emerged along the path. Scattered feathers covered the ground, some appearing as if plucked from a bird. Ahead, a torn piece of rope hung from a low-hanging branch, its frayed ends catching the light.

"What the hell happened here?" Ethan muttered, his voice tense with unease.

Maria stopped near a patch of flattened grass, crouching low. "Look at this," she said, shining her light on a faint set of tire tracks leading toward a small firepit. "Someone's been here recently."

Jonathan knelt beside her, his fingers tracing the disturbed earth. "They left in a hurry," he said. "No time to cover their tracks."

Ethan swept his flashlight across the area, his eyes widening as the beam revealed a sight that sent a chill down his spine. About ten small A-frame structures with green metal roofs stood in various stages of decay, their frames rotting and collapsing inward. The eerie stillness of the scene was unnerving, as if time were trying to erase this place.

"This place gives me the creeps. Where are we?" Ethan muttered, his voice heavy with disbelief.

"An old youth camp," Jonathan said, his gaze scanning the area. "Abandoned since the early '80s."

They moved cautiously into the abandoned camp, their flashlights cutting through the darkness as they surveyed the ruins. The area was eerily quiet, with remnants of its past life scattered around. Near one of the dilapidated structures, they discovered empty shell casings, the same caliber used in the horse shootings. A bloodied tarp lay crumpled on the ground, discarded carelessly. On a weathered picnic table, a handful of handwritten notes were scattered, their cryptic and fragmented writing hinting at something darker.

Maria leaned over the table, picking up one of the notes. Her brow furrowed as she read the jagged handwriting.

The blood – *it's everywhere.*

They come when the moon is low.

Don't speak. R.A.I.

Maria handed the note to Jonathan, her expression serious. He examined it closely, his jaw tightening as he read. "They were here recently alright," he said. "This is where they've been hiding to orchestrate the shootings."

The sharp crunch of broken glass echoed. The wolf reappeared, standing motionless beneath the rusted frame of a swing set, its swings long gone, leaving only the skeletal remains of the structure. Its ears twitched, and its fur seemed to bristle as if sensing danger. Without a sound, the wolf turned abruptly and vanished into the darkness.

Maria exhaled shakily, her voice breaking the silence. "Why do I get the feeling we're being watched?"

Jonathan's voice remained calm yet firm. "Because we probably are."

The unsettling silence enveloped them as they collected what evidence they could. The forest, once alive with the rustle of leaves and distant calls, now felt suffocating, as if it were holding its breath, waiting for something to occur.

Then, the faint buzz of Ethan's phone broke the silence. He pulled it from his pocket, squinting at the screen. "It's dispatch," he muttered, swiping to answer.

Maria and Jonathan paused, their attention shifting to Ethan as he turned away slightly to take the call. "Yeah, Wagner here… You got something?"

Jonathan crouched beside the bloodied tarp, his fingers brushing the dirt as if he were grounding himself while listening to Ethan's call. Maria stood by the crumbling doorframe of a nearby cabin, her arms crossed, her flashlight casting a steady beam over the cryptic note she had discovered moments earlier.

Ethan's shoulders stiffened. "Darryl Tompkins?" he said, his voice edged with disbelief and disgust. "You sure it's him? Yeah… Yeah, I'll follow up. Thanks."

He ended the call and turned back to the others, his expression grim. "The plate belongs to Darryl Tompkins," he said, sliding the phone into his pocket. "Dwayne Tompkins' brother."

Maria furrowed her brow. "Dwayne Tompkins… the poacher who wanted to kill the grizzly?"

Ethan nodded, the bitterness in his tone unmistakable. "Yeah. Let's just say the apple didn't fall far from the tree. He's kept a low profile for years but is dirty, just like his brother was. This isn't a coincidence."

Jonathan stood slowly, his eyes narrowing as the weight of the connection settled on him. "Dwayne's legacy," he said quietly, his jaw tightening with the implications. "He didn't just vanish when Dwayne turned up dead on the Black River. He and his people have been planning this, picking up right where his brother left off."

Maria sighed, the tension in her voice unmistakable. "So, what now? Do we report this to the county or keep pushing?"

Jonathan didn't respond immediately. The gentle trickle of the creek filled the night, its sound resembling the slow, inevitable drop of sand in an hourglass, reminding him that time was slipping away. He wasn't ready to give up – not after what they'd witnessed here – but the pieces of this puzzle had become far more dangerous than they'd anticipated.

"We push," Jonathan said finally, his tone decisive. "Darryl's not going to stop, and neither will we."

They had just begun discussing their next move when the sound of voices drifted toward them, faint at first but growing clearer. Carried by the breeze, they were followed by the crunch of boots on gravel. The unexpected noise caught them off guard, and Jonathan's head snapped toward it, his body tensing instinctively.

"Someone's coming," he whispered sharply. "Get down. Now."

They moved swiftly, extinguishing their flashlights and slipping into the shadows of the decaying cabins. Jonathan crouched behind a rotting wooden wall, with Maria and Ethan close behind. The three of them pressed against the splintered surface, their breathing reduced to near silence.

The voices grew louder and clearer now—gruff tones mingled with muffled laughter, the sharp kick of gravel announcing their approach. Jonathan's heart raced as the unseen figures entered the camp, each step echoing in the stillness. He raised a hand, signaling Ethan and Maria to stay low, his voice barely a whisper. "Guess we aren't alone after all."

Maria's heart pounded in her chest, each beat sounding impossibly loud against the eerie stillness of the camp. Ethan shifted slightly, peering around the corner of the wall they were hiding behind, his hand lingering near his pepper spray.

The footsteps grew closer, their cadence slow and deliberate. Whoever it was, they weren't trying to hide their presence. A beam of light swept across the picnic table where the cryptic notes had been. The figure halted, eyes narrowing as they realized the notes were missing.

His voice was sharp and irritated. "Someone's been here."

A second voice, deeper and chillier, responded with a hint of authority. "They won't get far. Spread out. Secure the area."

The voices grew louder as the flashlights swept closer, casting fractured beams of light across the debris-strewn floor. Jonathan pressed himself flat against the rotting wood, the damp scent of decay filling his nostrils. His heart hammered in his chest, and his ears strained to track the movement of the intruders.

One set of footsteps halted just outside the structure. Jonathan tightened his grip on the hunting knife at his side, his body coiled, ready to strike if necessary. Through the cracks in the wall, he could discern the faint glint of a rifle slung over the man's shoulder.

The voices suddenly converged by the creek. One man shouted, "Check over there!" while another cursed under his breath, shining a flashlight into the shadows.

Jonathan stole a glance at Maria and Ethan. Maria's jaw was tight, her hand resting on the holster at her side. Ethan's breath was shallow, his eyes darting toward the nearest escape route.

Seconds stretched into what felt like hours before one of the men called out, "It's clear. Let's move."

The beam of light swept past them one final time before vanishing completely. The sound of retreating footsteps mingled with the rustle of leaves and the faint gurgle of the creek. Jonathan waited until the silence became absolute before releasing a slow breath.

"They're gone," he whispered, his voice barely audible.

Ethan shifted, his muscles still tense. "For now," he muttered.

Maria stood, brushing off the dirt from her pants. Her eyes scanned the surrounding trees. "They'll be back. Whoever they are, they know this place, and they're not finished here."

Jonathan nodded grimly. "Neither are we. Let's move. We need to figure out who they are and what they're after."

VII: Montana Man

The group waited until sunrise before returning to the abandoned youth camp, as Jonathan insisted on waiting for daylight, fearing that the intruders might be nearby.

Morning light filtered through the dense canopy above Paradise Creek, casting dappled patterns across the forest floor. The creek trickled softly over the smooth stones, creating a deceptive calm against the tension lingering in the air. Jonathan stood at the water's edge, arms crossed, scanning the abandoned camp. Less than twelve hours ago, the site had been littered with damning evidence – now, it was eerily pristine.

Sheriff Clay Archer, a tall, weathered lawman from the Apache County Sheriff's Department, moved methodically through the area, jotting notes. His tan uniform and wide-brimmed hat blended into the earthy tones of the forest. Kneeling by the firepit, he ran a gloved hand over the undisturbed ground.

"You're saying there were shell casings, a tarp, and handwritten notes?" His voice was measured, withholding judgment.

"There were," Jonathan replied, his tone terse. "We wouldn't have called you otherwise."

Maria stood a few paces behind him, her arms crossed tightly over her chest. Exhaustion weighed heavily on her, but frustration was evident in her stiff posture. "Whoever was here had time to cover their tracks," she said, her voice tense. "They knew exactly what they were doing."

Ethan paced along the clearing's edge, his boots crunching on the gravel. "They didn't just clean up," he muttered. "They erased everything. No tarp, no casings, not a single tire track. It's as if last night never happened."

The Sheriff straightened, brushing his hands off before turning to face them. "If they were that thorough, they knew you'd be back," he said. "Whoever they are, they're organized and have the resources to make evidence disappear." He gestured toward the cold fire pit. "But without evidence, nothing links this place to the shootings – or anything else."

Jonathan's jaw tightened, frustration simmering just beneath the surface. He had encountered this before – cases where the criminals were always one step ahead, leaving only doubt and dead ends in their wake. "You know we're telling you the truth."

Sheriff Archer met his gaze without flinching. "Jonathan, you're a good man, and I don't doubt you," he said after a pause. "But belief doesn't hold up in court. If we're going to take these people down, we need more than just a tale of wolves and shadows."

Jonathan exhaled sharply through his nose, his hands resting on his hips as he turned toward the creek. Maria and Ethan exchanged a glance, both aware that Jonathan's frustration wasn't directed at the Sheriff – it stemmed from the sheer audacity of the operation they were beginning to unravel.

The Sheriff sighed. "I'll file a report, at least to keep an eye on this place. But for now, it's your decision on how to proceed. Just be careful - these people don't play by the rules."

Ethan let out a dry laugh, shaking his head. "That's the understatement of the year."

The Sheriff tipped his hat and walked toward his vehicle, the creak of his leather holster echoing with each step. "I'll be in touch if I hear anything. You do the same."

As the sound of his vehicle faded into the distance, the trio stood in heavy silence, the weight of the situation settling over them. The creek flowed peacefully, its serenity contrasting with the unseen danger lurking just out of reach.

Maria finally broke the silence, her voice tight. "Feels like we're chasing ghosts."

Jonathan turned to her, his expression grim yet determined. "They're not ghosts," he said. "They're real alright - flesh and blood. And sooner or later, they'll make a mistake. We just have to be ready when they do."

Ethan kicked at a loose rock with his boot, sending it tumbling into the creek. "Yeah, well, let's just hope their first mistake isn't putting us six feet under."

Jonathan's attention drifted upwards, where the creek met the rugged edges of Wyateé Meadow. "We'll figure it out. Let's head back to my place and regroup."

Without saying a word, the three of them ventured through the forest, seeking answers that seemed as elusive as the evidence that had vanished.

***

Back at Jonathan's cabin, the tension was palpable. The weight of their next move hung over them, unspoken yet heavy. Nestled among the towering pines, the cabin felt like both a refuge and a war room. Inside, the rich scent of freshly brewed coffee mingled with the smoky warmth of the crackling fire. Maps and notes sprawled across the wooden dining table, surrounded by empty mugs and crumpled pieces of paper – silent proof of their relentless search for answers.

As they pondered their next steps, Ethan's phone buzzed loudly on the table, shattering the heavy silence. He grabbed it, his brow furrowing as he answered.

"Wagner," he said curtly, his tone sharp.

When the call ended, his expression darkened. He looked up at Jonathan and Maria, his voice heavy. "The truck was spotted near a ranch on the Blue River. A rancher saw it parked along his property line this morning."

Jonathan straightened, his gaze intense. "Is anyone nearby?"

Ethan shook his head. "The rancher didn't stick around to find out, but the location lines up with Tompkins' usual territory."

Maria leaned against the table with her arms crossed tightly. "It's not just the truck," she said, tension lacing her voice. "It's a pattern. Every move they make is calculated—always one step ahead, leaving nothing behind. If we don't act now, this lead will vanish like all the others. We need to go."

Jonathan exhaled slowly, gripping the back of a chair. "We can't go in blind. We don't know what we're walking into, and that's a risk we can't afford to take."

Ethan's tone grew firm. "And if we don't go in, we're allowing them to slip further away. The clock's ticking, Crow. We're running out of time."

Maria glanced between them, her voice steady. "We need to make a decision. If we're serious about stopping them, this could be our only chance."

Jonathan's knuckles whitened on the chair as he grappled with the risks and urgency of the moment.

Ethan leaned forward, his focus unwavering. "I've already put a plan into motion," he said. "I knew we would eventually discover their location, but I couldn't allow you two to rush in blindly and get yourselves killed. I have an undercover agent coming from Phoenix. He'll survey the area and familiarize himself with the surroundings."

Jonathan arched an eyebrow, a smirk tugging at the corner of his mouth. "We aren't bringing some city slicker from the desert to play cowboy in these mountains."

Ethan didn't blink. "He's no city slicker. Grew up on a ranch in Montana. He knows what he's doing. Trust me."

Jonathan leaned over the table, his knuckles pressing into the worn wood as he glared at Ethan. "This is reckless," he said, his voice low yet firm. "You don't just send someone into a place like that without knowing exactly what you're dealing with. We don't even have solid proof they're there, let alone what they're up to."

Maria placed a hand on Ethan's, her voice steady yet resolute. "It's a good idea. These people know us – that's why we keep losing ground. We need someone on the inside."

Jonathan shook his head, his frustration etched across his face. "You're putting someone's life at risk. If this goes south, it's on us."

Ethan leaned forward. "I know the risks. So does Sam Reeves. He's trained for this."

Jonathan's scowl deepened, but he remained silent. Maria seized the moment to redirect the conversation back to the task at hand. "If we're doing this, it must be airtight. No one on that ranch can suspect he's anything but a drifter looking for work."

"Fine," Jonathan said, his tone rough. "But if anything feels off, we pull him out. No arguments."

Ethan and Maria nodded, and the group got to work. They crafted a backstory for Sam that would withstand scrutiny, debating every detail – his ranch hand experience, why he was drifting, and what brought him to Arizona. Maria suggested that the ranch where he worked had shut down due to mad cow disease—a solid explanation for why he relocated and was looking for work.

Ethan's expression was serious as he leaned in. "Sam will meet us at Molly Butler's tomorrow night to discuss the plan."

The stakes were high, and they all knew it.

***

The following evening, the team assembled at Molly Butler's Lodge, the warm glow from the windows spilling into the parking lot. Inside, the lodge hummed with quiet conversation, the rich aroma of prime rib and fruits of the forest pie lingering in the air.

Sam Reeves arrived twenty minutes late, pushing the wooden front door open with a confident stride – one that faltered slightly when he spotted the group in the bar. His appearance drew immediate reactions. He wore a bright red flannel shirt, crisp with pressed pleats, brand-new jeans, and immaculate snow boots that barely touched the dirt.

Ethan snorted into his coffee, struggling to hide his amusement. "Well, if we are hiring based on style, he'd be a shoo-in."

Jonathan sat with his arms crossed, raising an eyebrow as Sam approached. His gaze quickly shifted to the man's hands – smooth, meticulously manicured, more suited for handling paperwork than for ranch work.

"Evening," Sam said with an easy grin, pulling out a chair. "I hear you've got a job for me."

Jonathan didn't return the smile. "You look more like a runway model than a rancher."

Sam glanced down at his clothes, grin widening. "Figured I'd make a strong first impression."

Maria chuckled softly, shaking her head. "Oh, you made an impression, alright."

Jonathan leaned forward, skeptical. "This isn't a joke. If you don't look the part, they'll spot you as an outsider the second you step on that ranch."

Sam's grin faded as he sat up in his chair. "I understand the risks," he said, his tone growing serious. "I might not look the part yet, but I'm damn good at what I do. Give me the right tools and the right story, and I'll get it done."

Ethan leaned back, still smirking. "Where the hell did you get those boots?"

Sam's confidence remained steadfast. "Whatever it takes," he said, locking eyes with Jonathan. "I'm in this."

A waitress approached, smiling as she looked around the table. She turned to Jonathan and asked, "The usual?"

Sam was admiring the elk head mounted on the wall, he hardly recognized her presence. The waitress raised an eyebrow. "What's wrong? Did you leave a baby in the car?" Laughter erupted around the table, easing the tension just a bit. "I'll come back when you're ready," she said with a wink before greeting another table.

Jonathan shot Sam a look before nodding. "Alright, Sam. Let's see what you've got."

***

The following day, the team worked to make Sam look the part. They scoured thrift stores and consignment shops, trading his pristine red flannel for a weathered denim shirt and a battered Carhartt jacket. His new boots were scuffed and broken in, although Maria had to drag Ethan away from trying to smear them with cow patties.

"You want him to look rough, not smell like a feedlot," she said, yanking the boots away.

By the time they finished, Sam looked every bit like the down-on-his-luck drifter, complete with a dusty backpack filled with just enough supplies to seem believable without raising suspicion.

As Sam was getting ready to leave, Jonathan extended his hand. "Phone."

Sam hesitated for a moment before pulling it from his pocket. "Is this truly necessary?"

"If you're hitchhiking to the Blue River, you're likely not carrying a thousand-dollar phone," Jonathan said, slipping it into his own pocket. "It's about blending in. Stay in character."

Sam nodded, adjusting the strap on his backpack. "Got it."

Jonathan studied him for a moment, his face unreadable. "You know the plan. If anything feels off, you walk. No heroics."

"Understood," Sam said, his voice steady.

They drove him to a remote stretch of Devil's Highway 191, winding through the rugged landscape like a dark ribbon. The air was crisp, with the silence broken only by the occasional call of a raven or the distant rumble of a passing truck.

Sam climbed out of the vehicle, slinging his backpack over his shoulder. He turned back to the group, his expression calm yet determined. "See you on the other side," he said.

Jonathan watched him for a moment before giving a single nod. "Stay sharp."

As they drove away, Sam stood by the roadside, adjusting his pack and scanning the horizon. The wilderness stretched out before him—vast and unforgiving, a place where opportunity and danger walked hand in hand. With a steady breath, he started forward, his boots crunching on the lava rock as he made his way toward the ranch.

Then, the low rumble of an engine shattered the silence behind him. The sound grew louder with each step, causing his pulse to quicken. A truck rolled up slowly, its rusted fenders and battered frame unmistakable—the infamous blue truck.

Sam kept his head down, his stride steady, acting as if he hadn't noticed. His backpack hung loosely over his shoulder. The truck's tires crunched against the gravel as it slowed beside him, its brakes squealing high-pitched.

"Where you done headed?" a gruff voice called from the passenger's seat.

Sam turned, pretending to hesitate as he squinted into the afternoon sun. Behind the wheel sat Darryl Tompkins, his sharp, calculating eyes fixed on him. A younger man, equally rough-looking, leaned against the passenger door, suspicion etched on his face.

"Anywhere I can find work," Sam replied, shifting the weight of his pack. "Heard there's sum ranches 'round here that might need a good hand."

Darryl exchanged a glance with the other man, his expression unreadable. "What kinda work you lookin' fer?"

"Ranching," Sam said smoothly. "Been at it since I was a kid. Grew up in Montana, worked cattle most of my life. Ranch shut down 'cause of mad cow disease, so I hit the road."

The younger man snorted. "Montana, huh? What brings you down south?"

Sam shrugged, a faint smile on his face. "Heard Arizona's got work if you're willing to get your hands dirty. Figured I'd give it a shot."

Darryl's eyes narrowed, scanning him from head to toe. "You don't look like you been roadin' long."

Sam chuckled, pulling a weathered bandana from his pocket to wipe his forehead. "I guess I clean up better than most," he said with an easy grin. "But trust me, I've spent more nights under the stars than I'd like to count."

For a moment, the silence stretched, the two men in the truck sizing him up. Then, Darryl gave a sharp nod toward the bed of the truck. "Hop in. Let's see if you're worth keepin' 'round."

Sam nodded, tossing his bag while jumping into the bed of the truck. The truck lurched forward, gravel crunching under the tires as it roared down Devil's Highway.

As they approached the ranch, Sam noted the faded "*No Trespassing*" signs nailed to the fence posts – a clear warning to anyone who didn't belong. The property stretched for miles, dotted with weathered wooden buildings and open fields where cattle grazed; their low calls blended with the steady hum of the truck's engine.

As they pulled up to the main building, Darryl slid open the back window, his expression cold. "Listen close," he said. "You're here to work, not ask questions. You don't go near the other buildings, you don't talk to anyone, and you do what you're told. Understood?"

Sam nodded, his expression neutral. "Yes, sir."

The younger man smirked as he hopped out of the truck. "We'll see how long you last."

VIII: A Wolf Among Sheep

The first few days at the ranch passed in a blur of hard, backbreaking work. Sam shoveled manure, mended fences, and hauled heavy hay bales through the biting cold. He kept his head down, trying to blend in, yet his keen eyes never missed a thing.

Sam quickly realized that things didn't add up.

While working near the equipment shed one afternoon, he overheard a quiet conversation between Darryl and another man. Although their voices were soft, a few words were unmistakable – "the shipment" and "funds cleared." They weren't discussing cattle.

At night, trucks came and went at odd hours, their headlights slicing through the darkness as they rumbled down the dirt road. Sam caught fleeting glimpses of their cargo - crates covered with tarps, unloaded swiftly, and taken into one of the restricted buildings.

The ranch hands were equally peculiar. They seldom spoke to Sam; when they did, their responses were brief, and their demeanor tense. At mealtimes, conversations fell silent the instant he entered the room. Faces averted, voices hushed, a subtle yet unmistakable air of secrecy lingered.

Late one evening, feeling restless, Sam stepped outside to get a breath of fresh air. Near the far end of the property, he noticed a small group huddled closely together. Their voices were low yet tense, their body language rigid. One of them pointed toward the main road. Sam couldn't hear the words, but the tension was evident.

The next day, while mending a section of fence, Sam paused to stretch his sore back. His breath hung in the cold air as he cupped his hands around his face, warming it with his work gloves. As he glanced out over the rugged landscape, something in the distance caught his attention.

A pack of Mexican grey wolves emerged from the tree line, their sleek forms gliding swiftly across the open terrain. Sam froze, mesmerized. For a moment, everything else faded - the danger, the lies, the mission. He stood there, watching them, reminded of the raw, untamed beauty of the world beyond the ranch.

The pack paused, their heads swiveling as if sensing his presence. The alpha locked eyes with Sam, its golden gaze sharp and almost knowing. In that instant, an unspoken connection passed between them—an understanding that transcended words. Then, just as quickly, the wolves turned and disappeared into the trees.

Sam exhaled slowly, feeling the weight of the mission pressing down on him. The wolves reminded him of what was at stake and that he could not afford to fail.

Meanwhile, the atmosphere at the ranch had shifted. Sam could sense a change in how the others observed him—their stares lingering a moment longer, their glances sharper and more calculating. Conversations quieted when he walked by, and the easy banter he once shared with one of the hands had turned into cold stares and hushed whispers.

Darryl had become more watchful, his keen eyes observing Sam's every move. The other ranch hands followed his example, challenging Sam with subtle yet deliberate provocations.

"Hey, Montana," one of the men called out as Sam finished loading hay onto a truck. "What's the best way to handle a spooked steer?"

Sam wiped the sweat from his brow, keeping his voice steady. "Depends on the steer. But usually, you let it calm itself down. Rushing in just makes it worse."

The man nodded slowly, his expression neutral. "Not bad," he said, though there was something in his tone – it seemed too passive.

Later that evening, Sam sat alone in the bunkhouse, nursing a cup of coffee. The door creaked open, and a younger ranch hand entered, leaning casually against the doorframe. "Darryl wants to see you," he said, his voice dull.

A chill crept up Sam's spine, but he kept his expression neutral. "What for?"

The man shrugged. "Guess you'll find out."

The meeting was brief, yet the tension was undeniable. Darryl's questions were sharp, probing into Sam's background, with an undercurrent of warning in every word.

Leaning casually against his desk, Darryl locked eyes with Sam. "Have you ever heard the saying *'curiosity killed the cat?'*" he asked, his tone low and predatory.

Sam held his ground, replying evenly, "I'm just here to work. Not looking to stir the pot."

Darryl didn't respond immediately. Instead, a faint, humorless smile curled at his lips. "Good," he said finally. "Keep it that way."

IX: The Price of Curiosity

Johnathan steered his Land Cruiser west on Highway 260, the tires humming against the pavement as he ascended toward Antelope Mountain. He had just left Western Drug in Springerville, eager to head home, when movement on the hillside caught his attention.

A herd of bighorn sheep bolted across the ridge, their muscular forms moving in perfect unison, hooves kicking up dust as they fled. His instincts sharpened – something had startled them.

As he rounded the next bend, he saw it.

A thick column of black smoke curled into the sky just off the highway where routes 260 and 373 intersected. The orange flicker of flames licked through the dry grass, spreading quickly in the late-season wind.

Up ahead, a car was pulled over on the shoulder, and a lone traveler stood beside it, watching the fire grow larger. Jonathan pulled up next to him and rolled down his window. "Do you have a phone I can borrow?" he asked.

The traveler, a man with a New Mexico license plate, nodded and passed it over. Johnathan dialed the number for Greer Fire Department and waited.

"Greer Fire, this is Chief Hamilton."

"Chief, it's Crow," Jonathan said with a sense of urgency.

"Crow?" The chief sounded confused. "You calling me from New Mexico?"

"No, I'm borrowing a phone," Jonathan said quickly. "We've got a grass fire off 373 and 260. It's moving fast."

"Copy that. We're rolling," said the chief.

Jonathan returned the phone and jumped into his Land Cruiser. He had witnessed enough wildfires to understand how quickly they could spread, and there was no time to delay.

He turned sharply, throwing his truck into gear and smashed through the barbed-wire fence lining the road. The dry grass bent under the weight of his tires as he sped toward the flames. If he could tear up enough ground, he might be able to create a firebreak. Quickly, he performed tight circles and wide loops, spinning his tires against the grass to clear it away. The smoke burned his lungs, but he pushed on, cutting a scar into the dried vegetation.

Then, flashing lights.

Greer Fire arrived in a brush truck, sirens wailing. Five firefighters jumped out and moved quickly. One unrolled a thick hose while another connected it to the truck's side intake. A second firefighter pulled the pump lever, pressurizing the line.

Water blasted from the nozzle as the firefighters advanced, sweeping the flames with high-pressure streams. Another worked behind them, soaking the ground to prevent re-ignition. Steam hissed as the fire met the surge of water, and within minutes, the flames were subdued.

The fire chief turned to Jonathan, wiping the sweat from his shaved head. "Good thinking, tearing up the grass with your truck. That might have stopped it from jumping the road."

Johnathan smirked. "Well, figured it was either that or start chucking beer at it."

Chief Hamilton chuckled lightly. "Well, that would have been a damn shame."

At that moment, one of the firefighters jogged over, holding a small, partially burned fuel canister. He handed it to the chief.

"This was near the point of ignition," he said.

The chief studied it for a moment, his expression turning serious. Then he handed it back. "Put it back where you found it. We may have a crime scene here."

***

Two days later, Sam was working in the barn when he overheard a cryptic conversation – fragments about "a delivery" and "the Arizona crossing." It was the most promising lead he had encountered, too good to overlook.

He approached one of the ranch hands, keeping his tone casual. "What's all this talk about deliveries? Something big coming in?"

The man's eyes narrowed, his stance stiffening. "What're you asking for?"

"Just wondering," Sam quickly backpedaled. "Figured if there's a big shipment, we'd need to prep for it."

The man didn't respond. His expression darkened as he turned and walked away.

Minutes later, Sam found himself trapped in the barn. Three ranch hands stood in his path – Darryl at the front, arms crossed, his face contorted into a cold sneer.

"I knew something wasn't right about you," Darryl said, his voice thick with suspicion. "You got too many damn questions, Montana."

Sam took a slow step back, his pulse quickening. "I'm just doing my job," he replied, his voice on edge.

Darryl's sneer deepened, his eyes narrowing. "You've got a funny way of goin' about it. Let's see if you can answer a few more questions… the hard way."

The first blow struck from the side, slamming into Sam's ribs and knocking the wind out of him. He staggered but remained on his feet, instincts screaming at him to fight back – even though he knew he was outnumbered.

The situation escalated rapidly. Sam landed a powerful punch to one man's jaw; however, another tackled him from behind before he could react, slamming him hard against the barn wall. The punches came quickly and violently, each one making it evident that his cover was blown.

Darryl stood back, a cold smile spreading across his face as his men worked him over. "You want answers about deliveries?" he snarled. "Let me deliver a message: stay the hell out of my business."

By the time they finished, Sam was barely conscious, slumped against the barn's dirt floor. Darryl crouched beside him, gripping his collar. His voice was a low, menacing hiss. "You don't belong here. Take'm to the icebox."

Hours later, a frantic call came from a camper at the Blue Crossing Campground. Sam had been found near the tree line, barely clinging to his life. His eyes were swollen shut, his lip split, his clothes torn and soaked in blood. Jonathan, Ethan, and Maria didn't hesitate – they dropped everything and rushed to the campground.

"Stay with me, Sam," Ethan muttered, his voice strained as he knelt beside him, hands trembling as he checked for injuries.

Sam's eyelids fluttered open, his voice barely audible. "They know."

Jonathan's jaw tightened, and his face hardened with a mix of rage and guilt. "We need to get him out of here. Now."

They worked quickly, carefully lifting Sam into the back of Jonathan's Land Cruiser and securing him there. As they fastened him in, Maria's gaze caught something on the hill behind the campground.

A lone wolf stood at the ridge, its silver coat shimmering in the moon's glow. Its eyes – one icy blue, the other amber – locked onto hers for a lingering moment. Then, without a sound, it faded back into the shadows.

"It's him," Maria murmured, her voice tinged with awe.

Jonathan didn't respond; his focus was solely on getting Sam to safety. Ethan jumped into the passenger seat while Maria climbed into the back with Sam, applying pressure to his wounds as they sped toward the hospital in Springerville.

The drive was harrowing as the truck bounced over the uneven terrain while they raced against time. Maria's hands were slick with blood, her voice steady yet urgent. "You're going to make it. Just hang on."

Ethan kept his eyes on the road ahead, his fists clenched tightly in his lap. "This was not supposed to happen," he muttered.

Jonathan's grip on the wheel tightened, his expression stone-hard. "He'll be okay."

***

The hospital lights in Springerville were blinding as the emergency team rushed Sam inside to the trauma bay. The brand-new facility still had the sterile, untouched feel of a place that had just opened its doors.

An hour later, the trio sat in the waiting room, each on edge. Maria stared blankly at the wall, her hands still faintly stained with Sam's blood, a haunting reminder of what had just occurred. Ethan paced restlessly, frustration simmering just below the surface.

Jonathan sat away from them, his head bowed, the weight of the night pressing down heavily on his shoulders.

Finally, the PA emerged, concern etched on his face. "He's stable for now," he said. "However, his injuries are serious. We need to transfer him to a trauma center in Phoenix."

Jonathan gave a slow nod, his expression unreadable. "Do what you need to."

As the helicopter vanished into the night, its blades blending into the distance, the trio assembled in Western Drug's parking lot. The moon rested low over the mountains, casting long shadows across the asphalt.

Maria was the first to break the silence. "We need to reassess."

Ethan nodded, his jaw clenched. "They'll be on high alert now. This could be too big for us."

Jonathan gazed at the shadowy mountains, his expression resolute. "We keep moving forward," he stated firmly. "We owe it to the Chief."

X: The Summons

THE HOWL RIPPED through the village of Greer, deep and haunting, weaving through the pines like a ghost. It wasn't just a sound—it was a summons.

Jonathan's eyes quickly snapped open, his breath rapid and unsteady. Darkness enveloped him, thick with the haze of a fading dream. He sat up in bed, his joints aching in protest, and listened.

Nothing.

Had it been real?

He dragged a hand across his face, fingers grazing the rough stubble on his jaw. His breath remained uneven, and his heartbeat pulsated in both ears. If it was just a dream, why did it feel so real?

Swinging his legs over the edge of the bed, he pressed his bare feet against the chilly wooden floor. With a slow exhale, he pushed himself up, rolling his shoulders to relieve the stiffness of age and fatigue.

He moved to the bedroom window and pulled back the curtain. Moonlight bathed the treetops in silver, and the Little Colorado River glimmered in the distance. The meadow lay still, untouched by movement. Yet something was out there. He could feel it.

His fingers tightened around the worn fabric of the curtain – Marianne had sewn these long ago, her touch still lingering with every stitch. He had spent a lifetime reading the wilderness, trusting its signs – tracks in the mud, the wind shifting before a storm. But this…this was something different.

Dream or not, the call hadn't just woken him. It was a summons.

He couldn't ignore it.

The cabin door creaked as he stepped outside. The night air bit into his skin, cold enough to penetrate his heavy canvas jacket and settle deep into his joints. The scent of ponderosa pine hung heavily in the mountain air, mingling with the damp earth.

His Land Cruiser sat in the driveway, coated with a thin layer of frost. He pulled out his wallet, using his driver's license to scrape the ice from the windshield. The cold bit at his fingers, but he worked quickly, clearing just enough to see. Sliding into the driver's seat, he shivered against the icy leather. The engine rumbled to life, vibrations settling into his bones as he gripped the wheel.

He didn't know exactly where he was headed. But something deep inside was pulling him forward.

The headlights pierced the darkness as he ascended Northwoods Road, the towering pines pressing in around him. Lava rock crunched beneath his tires as he drove past the old railroad-grade bridge.

Then, a rock formation emerged.

His breath caught.

It was exactly as it had been in his dream.

Jagged and ancient, the stones rose from the earth like the ribs of a great beast, their surfaces worn smooth by time. Moonlight pooled in their crevices, casting deep, shifting shadows.

Jonathan shut off the engine, plunging the forest into silence.

Then, movement.

A flicker of silver at the edge of the tree line.

His grip on the steering wheel tightened, and his breathing paused.

In the darkness, a pair of glowing eyes blinked.

One blue. One amber.

The wolf.

It remained still, observing him with an unwavering gaze. The air between them felt charged, heavy with significance beyond comprehension.

It did not advance.

It did not retreat.

Then, as silently as it had come, it melted into the trees, vanishing like mist.

Jonathan exhaled, the weight of the moment settling deep in his chest.

Without hesitation, he stepped out of the vehicle and followed.

The soil beneath his boots was damp, softened by the cool night air. Each step released the rich, loamy scent of decaying leaves. Towering pines loomed above, their needles whispering in a language older than humanity, while slender aspens stood among them, their pale trunks resembling ghosts in the night.

A Pygmy Owl called from the darkness, its cry piercing through the stillness. Something quickly darted away in the underbrush, the snap of twigs marking its escape. Every sound felt magnified; the night was alive in a way Jonathan had never experienced before.

His fingers brushed against the rough bark of a tree as he steadied himself on uneven ground, the jagged texture anchoring him.

Then, something metallic caught his eye.

He crouched slowly, his knees protesting, and swept aside a low-hanging branch of leaves.

His stomach tightened.

It was an animal trap. Rusted and cruel, its steel jaws stretched wide, ready to snap shut on anything unfortunate enough to step on them. He ran his fingers along the corroded metal, tracing the jagged edges and the grime of old blood long since dried.

He straightened, his breath visible in the cold air. As he ventured deeper into the Apache-Sitgreaves forest, he discovered more – hidden beneath the brush, positioned along game trails, each placed with deliberate intent.

Jaw clenched, he seized a fallen tree branch and pressed it against the rusted metal. With a sharp crack, the trap snapped shut, echoing through the silence. He triggered them one by one, each violent clap shattering the stillness of the night.

This wasn't the work of amateurs.

A few yards ahead, something caught the dim light. He moved toward it, his pulse quickening.

At the base of a fallen tree lay a cache of supplies—crude yet unmistakable: makeshift ammunition, wooden boxes, spent bullet casings, and a waterproof bag containing documents, the paper distorted from exposure yet still legible.

Jonathan crouched, picking up one of the sheets. Scribbled notes. Numbers. Names he didn't recognize.

And then, at the bottom, something that made his blood run cold.

A set of coordinates.

Jonathan stared at them, his breath steady despite the fire growing in his chest. This wasn't merely poaching; it was something bigger – methodical and deliberate.

He looked up, scanning the darkness. The trees stood silent, indifferent to his discovery. But something else was watching.

A shift in the shadows. The faintest flicker of movement.

He wasn't alone.

He stood slowly, the papers clenched in his fist. His life had been built on tangible truths—what he could see, hear, and prove. Decades spent in these mountains had sharpened his instincts, and his survival was rooted in logic and skill.

But tonight, logic had led him here. And the wolf – Chief Grey Cloud – had guided him to something undeniable.

The man he was prior, practical and skeptical, would have dismissed it all. But the man standing here now, breathing in this cold air, holding irrefutable proof in his hands, couldn't deny what had happened.

Jonathan wasn't sure what to believe for the first time in his life.

But one thing was certain.

The hunt wasn't over.

And he wasn't turning back.

Moonlight spilled across the clearing like liquid silver, saturating the open space with an eerie glow. The air felt electric, heavy with something unseen yet undeniable. Jonathan stood motionless, the weight of the night settling deep in his chest. His heartbeat resonated like a steady drum, echoing the rhythm of Chief Grey Cloud's ritual.

Then, he felt it.

A presence.

The air shifted – an almost imperceptible disturbance, a ripple in the fabric of the night. He turned slowly.

Beyond the tree line, the wolf emerged yet again.

It moved like a shadow, silent and fluid, its silver coat gleaming in the moonlight. Its eyes—one blue, the other deep amber—fixed on him, filled with something beyond instinct.

Jonathan's fingers twitched by his sides. He should have felt fear or, at the very least, caution. But he didn't.

The wolf moved closer.

Jonathan exhaled, his breath misting in the cold. "You brought me here," he murmured, the words feeling foreign on his tongue as if they weren't completely his own.

The wolf's gaze remained steady.

This was no ordinary wolf, Jonathan knew that now. It was something more, something spiritual, something that had been in these mountains long before he arrived here.

Then, a gust of wind whispered through the clearing, causing the branches to sway. The wolf tilted its head slightly, then stepped forward again with slow, deliberate grace.

Jonathan's pulse raced, not from fear but from recognition.

"Chief," he breathed.

The name felt right, as if it had been waiting to be spoken.

The forest appeared to encroach upon them, the space between them charged with an unspoken energy. Jonathan had devoted his life to these mountains, understanding their ways and following their rhythms. Yet this felt different. This wasn't mere tracking; this transcended logic- it was something far more profound.

He was no longer just a man standing in the woods.

He was part of it.

The wolf held its gaze for a moment longer. Then, as silently as it had appeared, it turned. With a flick of its tail, it vanished into the trees, its silver coat dissolving into the darkness…a 'Grey Cloud' disappearing into the sky.

Jonathan exhaled slowly.

He understood now.

The land had been speaking to him all along; he simply hadn't been listening.

***

As the first light of dawn crept over Amberian Point, Jonathan returned to his cabin, his arms laden with evidence – items gathered from the hidden caches near Sheep's Crossing. A ledger filled with cryptic notes, spent bullet casings, and a torn scrap of cloth snagged on the rusted wire of an illegal trap.

He placed everything on the worn wooden table and exhaled, stepping back. The dim cabin light flickered, casting restless shadows on the log walls.

It all felt surreal.

Had he really wandered the wilderness in the dead of night? Had he truly followed a spirit? Or was it nothing more than a fevered dream – a trick of grief and exhaustion?

Jonathan ran a hand over his face, trying to distinguish reality from illusion. Dream or not, the evidence was indisputable. The traps, the ammunition, and the ledger were not fragments of his imagination. They were tangible. And tangible was something he could work with.

He reached for his old rotary phone, his fingers brushing against the faded 373 Greer Lodge sticker on the handle. The sight of it stirred up old memories – days spent with Marianne by the trout ponds, the scent of wood burning smoke, and the hum of laughter from the guests before the fire took it all away in 2011.

He spun the dial, and each number clicked methodically as it returned to its place. The line rang twice before a groggy voice answered.

"Wagner, here."

Jonathan glanced at the clock. "Sorry, I know it's early," he said. "I need you and Maria at The Rendezvous within the hour."

There was a beat of silence. Then Ethan sighed. "You're lucky I sleep with my boots on. You got something?"

Jonathan looked down at the pile of evidence.

"Yeah, I got something alright," he said.

Later that morning, the Rendezvous Cafe buzzed with quiet conversation, blending with the steady sizzle from the griddle. The air was thick with the aroma of fresh coffee and frying bacon.

Jonathan sat at a corner table with a manila folder in front of him. His fingers drummed idly against the tabletop while his black coffee remained untouched, steam curling into the air. He was lost in the tangled events of last night.

The bell above the door jingled, and he looked up to see Ethan and Maria step inside. Ethan's hair was still tousled from sleep, and Maria clutched a travel coffee mug as if it were the only thing keeping her upright.

Ethan dropped into the chair across from Jonathan, raising an eyebrow. "You better have a good reason for dragging us here so early."

Jonathan smirked. "I do."

Maria sat next to Ethan, adjusting her glasses on the bridge of her nose. "What's so urgent?"

Jonathan opened the folder and spread its contents across the table—bullet casings, a scrap of cloth, and, most importantly, the ledger.

Maria's eyebrows lifted. "Where did you get this?"

Jonathan leaned back, folding his arms. "The forest."

Ethan snorted. "Oh, well, that clears it right up."

Jonathan exhaled. "I followed the wolf."

Silence.

Maria shared a glance with Ethan. "Do you mean a literal wolf, or—?"

Jonathan shook his head. "No. I mean *him*. The Chief."

Ethan let out a low whistle. "And here I thought I was the only one sleep-deprived."

Jonathan ignored him, tapping a finger against the ledger. "Believe what you want, but it led me to this. And this changes everything."

Maria pulled the ledger closer, flipping through its worn pages. The handwriting was rough and hastily scrawled, yet clear enough—coordinates, names, supply orders—pieces of a puzzle waiting to be assembled.

"Jonathan, this is incredible. This could help build our case," she murmured, satisfaction growing in her expression.

Ethan picked up one of the bullet casings, rolling it between his fingers. "Same caliber as the ones used on the horses," he muttered. "We've got a direct link now."

Jonathan leaned in, his voice low and firm. "We need to figure out where those coordinates lead to. If we can track their movements, we might be able to get ahead of them."

Maria pulled out her phone and quickly entered the coordinates. A moment later, her brows furrowed. "These aren't just random locations; they follow a pattern—one near Wildcat, another by Three Forks."

Ethan glanced at the ledger. "You think this is a smuggling route? Alpine and Three Forks?"

Maria flipped through the ledger, her lips pressing into a thin line. "I do. These shipments. Look at the dates. The first recorded delivery coincides with when the illegal traps began appearing. The second aligns with the first confirmed horse shooting, and this one is the abandoned youth camp." She ran her finger down the page. "And this last one…just a few days ago near Sheep's Crossing. Whoever is behind this is working on a schedule. Someone is coordinating these deliveries."

Ethan leaned back, arms crossed. "Alright, so we know someone is supplying these guys. But that doesn't explain why they are killing horses. There's no black market demand for mustangs."

Jonathan's jaw tensed. "Unless they weren't the targets."

Ethan's brow furrowed. "What do you mean?"

Jonathan tapped the bullet casing beside his coffee cup. "What if the horses were simply in the way? Consider where they were shot—prime land near water sources and trails deep enough to conceal the activity. You both mentioned it didn't seem like poaching. Perhaps that's because it wasn't. Maybe someone was clearing the land for another purpose."

Maria sat back, her gaze sharpening. "That… actually makes sense. If you want to keep people away from an area, killing wild horses would only draw attention. Locals would chalk it up to reckless poaching. Meanwhile, something else is happening away from the crime scene."

Ethan exhaled slowly. "Alright. But what? What the hell are they trying to do out here?"

Maria grabbed the ledger again, flipping to another section. "Look at this," she said, pointing to a set of coordinates listed alongside various shipments. "These numbers match locations where we've already found traps and illegal caches. But these—" she tapped another set, "are farther north, closer to the reservation border near Mount Baldy."

Jonathan studied the numbers. "Whatever they're up to, they're moving south - closer to Maverick."

Ethan shook his head. "If this were just about poaching, they wouldn't risk getting this close to federal and tribal land. They'd stay hidden."

Maria's eyes wandered to the torn cloth, the stitched 'T' still visible. She exhaled as she met Jonathan's gaze. "Which brings us right back to Darryl Tompkins."

Jonathan nodded. "His brother ran one of the largest poaching rings in the White Mountains for over a decade. Then, after we rescued the grizzly, his body was suddenly found floating in the Black River. But Dwayne wasn't just dealing in illegal game—he was trafficking fentanyl, using remote areas to transport goods people weren't supposed to see. What if Darryl picked up where his brother left off?"

Ethan's expression darkened. "Smuggling."

Maria exhaled. "If that's true, then this isn't about wildlife at all. It's about the land. They're using it as a corridor."

Jonathan set his jaw. "Which means we're not dealing with a handful of reckless poachers. This is about control—who moves through these mountains without being seen. The horses, the wolves, any sign of conservation efforts… they're all obstacles."

Ethan leaned forward, rubbing his temple. "Jesus. This means whoever is behind this thing is thinking long-term. If they're using this area for transport, they're making damn sure no one pays attention."

Maria stared at the ledger. "It could involve drugs, weapons, or even human trafficking. We need to figure out who's financing this."

Jonathan nodded. "And to do that, we follow the supply chain."

Silence settled over the table as the weight of their realization sank in. Then Ethan exhaled, leaning in. "Alright. What's our move?"

Maria flipped through the ledger. "These shipments didn't just appear out of nowhere. If we can trace where they're coming from, we'll find the people funding this operation."

Jonathan tapped the table. "That supply cache I found last night - some of the boxes had Darryl Tompkins' name on them. If we can get the sheriff's office to check it out, we might be able to link him directly to the operation."

Ethan leaned back in his chair, rubbing a hand over his face. "That's a big 'if.' What if they've got people inside law enforcement?"

Maria nodded. "Which means we can't go to just anyone. We need to go straight to the Sheriff."

Ethan frowned. "And what if they brush us off?"

Jonathan's expression hardened. "Then we find another way to make them listen."

Ethan smirked, shaking his head. "You always have a backup plan, don't you?"

Jonathan took a slow sip of coffee. "After all these years? Damn right, I do."

The cafe was busy, the low hum of conversation started to blend in with the clatter of plates. Fresh cobbler wafted through the air, anchoring them to their seats.

Then, Maria checked her watch. "We should get moving."

Ethan stretched and stood. "I'll call in a favor, see if those shipments ever passed through a border checkpoint."

Jonathan pushed back his chair and adjusted his jacket. "I'll take the evidence to Sheriff Archer. If he's serious about shutting this down, he'll take action."

Maria hesitated. "And if he doesn't?"

Jonathan's gaze drifted toward the window, his eyes fixed on the meadow. "Then we know whose team he is on."

As they stepped outside into the cool, late-morning air, a familiar presence stirred the edges of Jonathan's awareness.

The wolf stood at the edge of the Little Colorado River, just past the brown cabin across the street.

Its silver coat shimmered softly in the dawn light, and its mismatched eyes—one blue, one amber—focused on him with quiet intensity.

It had led him to the truth.

And now, it was watching. And waiting.

Jonathan held its gaze for a long time before the wolf turned and vanished into the willows.

Ethan followed his line of sight. "You see something?"

Jonathan exhaled, a small smile forming. "Just an old friend."

Ethan chuckled. "You and your ghosts, man."

Jonathan didn't respond. He stepped into his Land Cruiser and closed the door.

XI: Stand or Fall

THE FIRST LIGHT OF DAWN spilled over Escudilla Mountain, painting the sky with shades of deep orange and soft blue. Mist lingered in the valley below, drifting through the dense pines like a wandering spirit.

Jonathan tightened his rifle strap and scanned the tree line beyond the compound. This was it—the moment they had spent weeks preparing for. Behind him, team members murmured as they settled into their final positions.

The USFWS, AZGFD, and the Apache County Sheriff's Department assembled in full force. This confirmed what Jonathan, Ethan, and Maria had suspected for weeks—this mission was too vast for them. The smuggling, wildfires, and dead horses all indicated something far greater than a small band of poachers from Alpine. They needed backup.

A few feet away, Ethan stood rigid, his usual easygoing demeanor replaced by a sharp focus. His hand rested on his sidearm, and his eyes were fixed on the compound below. The wooden buildings stood at the edge of a clearing, their shadows stretching sideways into the morning light.

The place was silent – too silent.

Maria checked her radio, speaking to a Sheriff's deputy in hushed tones. Despite her composed expression, Jonathan noticed the slight tension in her grip as her fingers clutched the radio a bit too tightly. The mission was high stakes, and they all felt it.

Ethan exhaled sharply and turned to Maria. "Stay back with the Sheriff's team. If anything goes wrong, we need someone to coordinate the operation."

Maria arched a brow at him. "You're telling me to stay behind?"

Ethan hesitated, then exhaled. "I just want you to be safe."

She held his gaze for a long moment before her expression softened. "I know."

Ethan took a steady breath. "Maria, I love you." The words hung heavily in the cold air, yet his voice remained unwavering.

Maria blinked, then let out a small, breathy laugh, shaking her head. "You pick *now* to tell me that?"

"I have terrible timing, I know," Ethan admitted, a faint smile tugging at his lips despite the situation.

Maria reached out and squeezed his hand. "I love you too." Then, with a hesitant nod, she stepped back toward the sheriff's team.

Standing just far enough to give them space, Jonathan glanced over at Ethan. "You ready?"

Ethan rolled his shoulders, the moment of tenderness giving way to the weight of the mission. "Yeah. Let's end this."

The radio crackled. "Briggs USFWS here. We're in position. We move on your command."

Jonathan lifted his binoculars, surveying the compound one last time. Then, on his radio, he said, "Move in."

Floodlights instantly blazed to life, cutting through all the shadows. A booming voice rang out over a megaphone. "Apache County Sheriff's Department! Come out with your hands up!"

For a moment, nothing.

Then, chaos erupted.

A group of ranchers burst from the main building, scattering in all directions. Some sprinted for the trucks, while others bolted toward the tree line. Jonathan caught a glimpse of Darryl Tompkins heaving a large crate into the bed of a blue truck before jumping into the driver's seat.

"They're running!" Ethan shouted.

"Cut them off before they hit the tree line!" Briggs barked into his radio.

Jonathan and Ethan sprinted toward their vehicle while deputies and game wardens chased the others on foot. Gravel erupted beneath spinning tires as the trucks tore away from the compound, racing toward the winding backroads that led to Escudilla Mountain.

Jonathan slammed the truck into gear as they took off in pursuit. "They're heading toward Forest Road 56," he muttered, gripping the wheel tighter.

Ethan, in the passenger seat, adjusted his rifle. "They're trying to lose us in the backcountry."

The chase was on.

Law enforcement vehicles sped down the winding dirt road, kicking up clouds of dust as they maneuvered through the tall pines. However, something about their driving troubled Jonathan. They weren't merely fleeing – they were leading them somewhere.

His grip on the wheel slightly loosened. "They're headed towards Profanity Tank."

Ethan shot him a look. "Bad place for a shootout."

Jonathan nodded grimly. "We need to stop them before we get that far."

Ahead, the lead truck took the corner too quickly, its tires sliding on the loose gravel. It swerved wildly before fishtailing into a ditch with a jarring thud. The doors quickly flew open, and men spilled out – some armed, others frantically unloading cargo.

Jonathan slammed the brakes, tires skidding as he swerved to avoid colliding with the truck in the ditch. The sheriff's convoy pulled up beside him, dust swirling in their wake.

Briggs stepped out of his vehicle, gun drawn. "Nobody move!"

Darryl Tompkins stumbled back, a crate slipping from his grip and crashing to the ground. He turned to Briggs, raising his hands to surrender. But beside him, a figure stepped forward – broad shoulders, weathered, and too damn familiar.

Sheriff Clay Archer.

Except he wasn't in uniform. He was dressed in torn jeans, a faded flannel shirt, and scuffed boots, he looked more like a rancher than the lawman they had met at Paradise Youth Camp. But there was no mistaking that it was him.

Jonathan's breath caught in his throat. The sheriff – the man they had trusted – wasn't just involved. He was the mastermind.

The group stood frozen, disbelief flickering across their faces.

Archer let out a slow, amused chuckle. "What's the matter? You act like you've seen a ghost."

A shot rang out.

Then another.

The sharp crack sliced through the air, quick and lethal. Jonathan barely had time to react before more gunfire erupted, echoing through the canyons and ravines.

"Take cover!" Ethan's voice crackled through the radio, barely audible over the thunder of boots pounding against the earth. Johnathan and the others dove behind a jagged outcrop of boulders, their hearts hammering. The ground trembled beneath them – a harsh reminder of the danger closing in.

The criminals weren't running. They were fighting back.

Jonathan crouched low, his back pressed against the rough rock, breathing shallowly. The wind hurled through the trees and the weight of a watchful osprey broke a branch from above. For a moment, nature held its breath. Then -

Another shot - close. So close he felt the heat graze his cheek.

He exhaled slowly, forcing himself to focus. The criminals knew this terrain well. It was easy for them to slip between rocks and disappear into gullies where law enforcement's heavy gear would hinder their pursuit. This wasn't just about stopping them; it was about protecting the mountain, the horses – everything was at stake.

"We need to move," Jonathan muttered to Ethan.

Ethan nodded, his expression grim and his eyes fixed on the landscape ahead. Without another word, they pressed on, pursuing Archer. Though he was an established hunter in the area, Jonathan knew this mountain well, and he was determined to catch him.

As they ascended Escudilla Mountain, the air thinned, and Profanity Ridge cut across the darkening sky. The terrain stretched out before them – an unforgiving expanse of rock, scrub, and rotting trees from the Wallow Fire. Every step demanded more – more strength, more breath, more resolve.

Jonathan pressed on, beads of sweat forming on his forehead as he moved with practiced precision. The mountain wasn't just their battlefield; it was their reckoning.

Ethan trailed closely, his figure barely discernible against the vast terrain. He knew Jonathan wouldn't allow Archer to escape, but time was running out. Every wasted second brought them closer to permanently losing these criminals.

"Can you see him?" Ethan asked, his voice tight with urgency.

Jonathan shook his head, scanning the landscape as his eyes flicked from one boulder to the next. This had become more than a chase; it was a test of endurance, a battle of wills. Archer held the advantage. He knew this mountain, learned how to disappear into the landscape, and used the terrain to his benefit.

Jonathan narrowed his eyes as he adjusted his pack, his senses heightened. Then, in the distance, he caught sight of it—movement, fleeting yet unmistakable. His pulse quickened. A figure, barely visible against the rock face as it slipped between two boulders.

"There!" Jonathan hissed, pointing.

Without waiting for a response, he lunged forward as his legs burned from the strain of the ascent. The ground beneath was treacherous – loose rock and uneven footing.

He skidded to a halt at the edge of a dry creek bed, his breath sharp with measured pulls. Milk Creek. The place where Arizona's last grizzly had fallen in 1932. As the dust blew, it looked like a ghost whipping across the mountain.

Ethan followed closely behind him, but as they approached Archer's position, the danger significantly increased. Jonathan's pulse raced, each step echoing louder than the distant gunfire below.

This was no longer about just stopping Archer.

This was something more significant – it was about survival. The legacy of the Mexican grizzly had united them, compelling them to resist those who would otherwise see the animal erased.

And then, through the trees, he saw them.

Two massive forms moved through the underbrush, silhouetted against the fading twilight. Mexican grizzlies.

Jonathan's heart skipped a beat. He had heard rumors that they had returned to the mountain where they had once roamed. But seeing them here and feeling their presence in the wild made everything snap into place.

Ethan stopped beside him, following his gaze. "Do you think...?"

Jonathan didn't answer immediately. He couldn't. His mind was still processing what lay before them. The bears – their sheer presence – reminded him of everything at stake.

The bears moved with quiet confidence, unperturbed by their presence as they grazed on wild berries. Jonathan swallowed hard; the wind parched his throat as he nodded. "They're here. Because of us."

The sight of the grizzlies seemed to fuel Jonathan's determination. But Archer had not stopped moving, and neither could they.

"Come on," Jonathan muttered, pushing forward.

The grizzlies represented more than mere animals—they had become a symbol. They serve as a reminder of their purpose and the struggles they endured—the past, the mission, and everyone who believed in them.

But Clay Archer wasn't part of that picture. *He was part of the problem.*

The chase continued deeper into the heart of the mountain, with the terrain becoming more treacherous with every step. The air thinned further as they reached 10,000 feet in elevation, and the setting sun formed shadows across the peaks, transforming the rocky slopes into an unforgiving labyrinth.

Jonathan's muscles burned, exhaustion gnawing at him, yet he refused to slow down. Archer was just ahead, somewhere in the maze of stone and shadow, and if they didn't move now, he would vanish into the wilderness for good.

Then, the path opened – a sheer drop at the cliff's edge.

Clay Archer stood there, silhouetted against the bruised sky – the man who had betrayed the sheriff's department and orchestrated the destruction of everything they had fought to protect.

With his back to the void, he didn't flinch. He was calm, almost unnervingly so, leveling the barrel of his rifle toward their direction.

Johnathan could hear his ragged breath from the chase and see the slight tremor in his hands—not from fear, but from something else—something more profound and darker.

"Stay back!" Archer barked, his voice trembling with desperation. His gun was steady, but his body was tense, coiled like a spring ready to snap.

Johnathan stood resolute, his rifle raised, yet he did not fire.

Archer let out a harsh, bitter laugh. "You truly don't understand, do you?" His lip curled in disgust. "These damn wolves and horses. They don't belong here! The government reintroduced the wolves, and now they're killing off our cattle, pushing out herds, ruining everything my family has built."

His voice cracked, rage simmering just beneath the surface. "And those feral horses are destroying the land where our cattle have grazed for a century!"

Jonathan met Archer's glare with a steady, measured look. His voice was calm yet firm.

"Clay, the environment has changed, just like everything else. The wolves and the horses aren't controlling anything – they're just trying to survive, like you and me."

Archer laughed, producing a harsh, bitter sound, his finger resting on the trigger. "You talk about wildlife as if I care. You want to talk about saving them, but you're all the same—just parasites, draining the land dry. My father knew it. And his father before him."

Jonathan's pulse quickened as his grip tightened on his rifle. There was no reasoning with Archer; he could see it in his eyes, that unshakable, twisted conviction. This wasn't about cattle. It was about greed, power, and control.

"The damn animals don't care! They've been ours to use since the dawn of time!" Archer roared. "What good are these oversized rodents if you can't warm your feet with them?!"

Ethan's voice cut through the tension, sharp and focused. "Clay, it doesn't have to end like this. We don't want anyone to get hurt."

"Like hell! If you think I'm going down without a fight, you're mistaken, pal!" Archer snapped, cocking the gun and leveling it at Ethan.

Ethan didn't flinch. "Surrender now, and you'll face justice." His stance shifted slightly, ready to make a move if needed. "The law already has you surrounded. There is no escaping this."

Archer let out another laugh, eyes burning with defiance. "You think they'll just lock me up? Let me rot in a cage like some damn animal?" He shook his head, taking another step back, boots skimming dangerously close to the cliff's edge.

His gaze rotated between them, wild and unwavering. "You want to stop me? You'll have to kill me first."

Then, there was a pause—an awful stillness.

The world seemed to narrow to the gleam of Archer's crazed eyes and the rifle in his hands. Nothing moved except the wind, whipping through their clothing and kicking up dust around their boots.

Jonathan's mind was racing. He couldn't let Archer escape. But how far was he willing to go to stop him?

The moment continued to stretch, and every heartbeat pounded in his chest. He could feel the weight of it—the tension, the fear, Marianne. Everything had led to this.

Then, Archer moved. The rifle came up again.

Jonathan's pulse surged. Instinct screamed at him to fire – to end it before Archer could – but something held him back. Once he crossed that line, there would be no going back. And deep down, a quieter truth anchored him – Marianne. The thought of her, of what he had lost and what remained, cut through the chaos. He couldn't lose himself to this. Not like this.

"Don't do it, Archer!" Ethan shouted, voice pleading.

But it was too late.

The rifle was aimed, finger tightening on the trigger. Jonathan didn't think – he lunged.

The shot rang out.

A deafening crack as the bullet struck a rock beside him, shards flying in all directions. Backed up against the ledge, Archer was desperate.

It was a warning shot.

Jonathan and Ethan didn't flinch. They couldn't afford to. The air was thick with tension, every second ticking towards the inevitable. They moved in sync, each aware that one wrong step could be their last.

Archer remained too close to the cliff's edge. Jonathan's eyes darted to the terrain, noting the loose rock beneath his feet—there was no safe way to rush him without risking another shot.

But there was a way.

Ethan gave him a nod—brief, sharp. The plan was set.

In an instant, they moved. Jonathan feigned left, drawing Archer's attention, while Ethan struck low, as quick as a viper. The distraction was sufficient. Archer's focus wavered as hesitation flickered across his face.

Jonathan lunged.

His boot swept Archer's legs out from under him, sending him crashing to the ground. The rifle flew from his grip, skidding across the rock before tumbling over the cliff's edge.

Archer let out a strangled yell as he pitched toward the drop, his arms flailing for something – anything – to grab. But Jonathan was already there.

"Let go!" Archer snarled, but Jonathan only tightened his grip.

"Not a chance," Jonathan growled. With a single grunt, he hauled Archer back, every ounce of strength focused on pulling him to safety.

Ethan appeared in an instant, securing handcuffs around Archer's wrists with practiced speed. It was over.

"You're done, Archer," Jonathan said, his voice low. "This is over."

All the criminals from the ranch were finally in custody. Law enforcement moved in swiftly, apprehending Archer and his men. Jonathan stood silently, observing as the weight of it all settled over him.

The damage was overwhelming – wildlife killed, habitats destroyed. And for what? Greed. Power. Profit has never cared for the land, the animals that belonged here, or the people who fought to protect them.

Maria stepped up beside Ethan, holding his hand. "This is going to take years to undo."

Jonathan nodded, wiping sweat from his brow. He didn't need to say anything; Maria's words spoke the truth. Yet, there was a grim determination on her face that echoed his own.

The three stood together, with Escudilla Mountain casting a long shadow over the land. The sun was setting, but the day felt lost – a victory that resonated hollowly.

Ethan embraced Maria in a brief, firm hug. She held on for a moment, a silent understanding passing between them. Jonathan observed from a step away, a faint smile touching his lips – yet it never fully reached his eyes.

"It's over," Maria whispered as she stepped back, but her eyes remained distant. "But the fight never really ends, does it?"

Ethan exhaled, glancing toward Jonathan before nodding. "No. It doesn't."

The criminals were taken away in handcuffs, silent and defeated. The trio remained behind, standing as the last light faded from the horizon. There were no cheers, no sense of triumph—only a quiet understanding of what had transpired.

Then, from the edge of the trees, a figure emerged.

A wolf.

Maria inhaled sharply. "It's the Chief."

The wolf stepped forward, moving with quiet, steady grace, its presence both familiar and otherworldly. It neither snared nor bared its teeth or moved or fled. Instead, it stood with them as if it had always belonged.

Jonathan exchanged glances with Ethan, neither daring to speak. The air was thick with something unspoken, something ancient. It wasn't just an animal standing with them—it was a presence, a guide.

Maria took a slow step forward, her voice barely above a whisper. "You stayed with us."

The wolf's ears flickered, its gaze shifting between them as if memorizing their faces. For a long moment, they existed together – man and beast, past and present woven together.

Then – the shift.

A low growl emanated from the wolf's chest. Its lips curled back, revealing its teeth in the dim light. Jonathan's breath caught as the brown eye shifted. The ember hue gracefully melted into a glacial blue, transforming the two eyes into radiant orbs of bright azure. The Chief was gone.

The wolf's muscles tensed, and in an instant, it bolted, vanishing into the darkness, swallowed by the wild.

Jonathan exhaled, watching the spot where the wolf had disappeared, feeling the finality settle into his bones. "The Chief has moved on. He no longer resides in the wolf."

Ethan glanced at him, then at Maria, his voice quiet. "Where has he gone?"

Jonathan didn't respond immediately. He gazed up at the stars. Finally, he said, "Where he's always been. The spirit world."

XII: New Roots

LATE THE NEXT DAY, the air had warmed, though it still carried the lingering scent of freshness throughout the valley. Johnathan dipped a brush into the bucket of stain, the thick, honey-colored liquid clinging to the bristles as he swept it methodically across the log cabin's exterior, allowing the rich color to soak into the aged wood.

It was slow work, but he didn't mind. He and his wife had built this place with their own hands decades ago, hand-hewing each log into something solid that could withstand the test of time. The cabin was more than just a shelter; it was a part of him, a piece of his history etched into the landscape of Greer, nestled between the towering ponderosas and the rolling meadows of the White Mountains.

The rhythmic sweep of the brush against the wood was familiar, even meditative, but his thoughts were anything but settled.

His body ached from the past few weeks—shoulders tight, knees stiff each time he crouched to reach the lower course of logs. Despite being in his sixties, his strength hadn't abandoned him, but today...today, the years felt heavier than they had in a long time. His broad, calloused hands, marked by a lifetime outdoors, flexed around the brush, the stain seeping into the creases of his skin.

Staining the logs was an act of preservation—a way to protect what time and the elements would eventually wear down.

Just like Chief Grey Cloud.

Jonathan exhaled and set the brush against the bucket's edge. He straightened, rolling his shoulders to ease the stiffness in his back, but the ache in his heart remained. Chief Grey Cloud had been as steady and enduring as the mountains themselves. His passing still weighed on Jonathan, lingering like unfinished business.

A sound behind him—gentle footsteps crunching on pine needles, scarcely disturbing the peace.

Jonathan turned, wiping his hands on a stained rag. A familiar figure stood at the edge of the yard, framed by sunlight filtering through the trees.

Bidzil.

The young Apache man stood tall and lean, his long black hair tied back at the nape of his neck. His features were sharp yet calm, and his deep brown eyes reflected the same quiet intensity his father once possessed. He wore a faded flannel over a dark shirt, and his jeans were dusted from the road.

Jonathan hadn't seen him since the ceremony.

"Bidzil." Jonathan nodded to greet him.

Bidzil approached, his gaze drifting over the half-stained logs before settling on Jonathan. "It seems you've got your hands full."

Jonathan huffed a quiet chuckle. "Never ends. Wood'll rot if you don't take care of it."

Bidzil stopped a few feet away, his expression unreadable. "That's why you're here in this life, Jonathan. To take care of things."

"Well, I don't know about that. What brings you to Greer?" Johnathan asked.

Bidzil hesitated, then looked away for a moment as if weighing his words. "I felt it," he finally said, pointing at his chest. "The moment his spirit left this world. When the eyes change."

Jonathan didn't need to ask what he meant.

The wolf.

Bidzil exhaled, his shoulders rising and falling with each breath. "For so long, I believed he would always be a part of this land. No matter how the world changed, my father would remain a constant."

Jonathan nodded, the image still vivid in his mind. The mismatched eyes watched over them before fading into the forest. "He was ready," he murmured.

Bidzil's jaw tightened. "The tribe... they're asking me to take his place." He let the words settle as if testing how they felt spoken aloud. "They want me as Tribal Chairman."

Jonathan met his gaze. "Is that what you want?"

For the first time, Bidzil appeared uncertain. He shifted, tucking his hands into his pockets. "I don't know if I can live up to him."

Jonathan closed the lid on the bucket. "No one can."

Bidzil looked up, his brow creasing.

Jonathan sighed. "Your father wasn't the Chief because he filled someone else's shoes; he was the Chief because he walked his own path. You're not meant to be him, Bidzil. You're meant to be you."

Bidzil remained silent for a long moment. Then, he offered a slight nod, gazing past Jonathan toward the valley beyond the cabin. "I told them it was my honor to serve our people."

Jonathan nodded, sensing there was more.

Bidzil stepped forward, his voice steadier now. "I want to invest in education, preserve our language and stories, and strengthen the connection between our past and future generations. If I do this, I want it to matter."

Jonathan studied him, then gave a slow nod. "Then that's exactly what you should do."

Something sparkled in Bidzil's gaze – relief. Or perhaps it was the thought of stepping into something far more significant than himself.

The wind rustled through the trees, causing pinecones to tumble to the ground, where they cracked against the soft bed of pine needles.

Jonathan glanced at the unfinished logs he had sanded, then back at Bidzil. "Lend me a hand?"

Bidzil smirked, shaking his head. "I knew if I came here today, you'd put me to work."

Jonathan handed him a brush. "As your father once said, 'Idle hands let the wind carry them away.'"

They both laughed.

They worked in silence for a while, the steady rhythm of their brushes filling the air. The scent of fresh stain mingled with the raw earthiness of the sanded wood.

After a few minutes, Bidzil spoke again. "My father respected you. He never said it, but he didn't have to."

Jonathan kept focused on the wood. "I respected him too."

Bidzil hesitated, then added, "And I believe he is sitting with Marianne today. They are both guarding you."

Jonathan exhaled, his gaze drifting to the mountains overlooking the Little Colorado River. New aspen growth filling the void left by the Wallow fire, serving as a quiet reminder of resilience. The land felt different now—not empty, not broken—just changed.

As the sun climbed higher over the trees, Jonathan found himself hoping—just maybe—that this marked the beginning of something new.

***

The scent of seared steak and wood smoke lingered in the air as Jonathan stepped through the doors of Molly Butler's Lodge. The place had been around for over a century, its walls still soaked in stories, laughter, and the murmurs of tired hikers and ranchers seeking a warm meal after a long day in the mountains.

Dim lantern-style lighting cast a warm, golden glow across the interior, where wooden walls featured paintings by a local artist, old photographs of Greer, and books for sale by Wink Crigler. It was the kind of place where time slowed, the chill of the outside world faded, and the warmth inside came not only from the fire but also from the people who gathered there.

Jonathan noticed Ethan and Maria at the long table in the back of the bar, where the soft yellow light from above pooled on their table. Above the bar, a muted replay of a Chicago Cubs game played on the television.

Ethan sat with his arms crossed, one boot resting on his opposite knee, appearing more at ease than he likely felt. His deep brown hair was slightly tousled as if he had run his hands through it one too many times. He had a look that could be brooding if not for the permanent glint of mischief in his eyes.

Maria sat beside him, her back straight, wearing a loose-fitting olive-green sweater that blended with the lodge's rustic tones. She emanated quiet thoughtfulness, her fingers lightly wrapped around her glass of water, but Jonathan knew that mind of hers was always at work.

As Johnathan approached, Ethan looked up with a smirk. "Well, look who finally decided to show up. We were just about to send out a search party."

Jonathan sat on the stool across from him. "You're about five jokes away from being funny."

Ethan grinned, unfazed. "That's the spirit."

The waitress approached, setting down a round of drinks—two beers and a whiskey neat. Jonathan nodded in thanks, his hand closing around the glass. The room's warmth, the weight of the past few weeks, and the simple act of sitting here with these two settled into his bones all at once.

For a while, they didn't speak.

The comfortable silence stretched between them, heavy with unspoken words that didn't need to be said yet still awaited acknowledgment. This adventure transformed them, not just as individuals but as a cohesive team. They had emerged on the other side but at a cost.

Finally, Maria broke the silence. "So… now what?"

Ethan let out a low whistle, shaking his head. "Hell of a question." He leaned forward, absentmindedly tracing the condensation on his glass. "We just took down an entire crime ring, and yet what's bothering me the most is…" He exhaled sharply, shaking his head again. "That damn wolf."

Maria nodded, her gaze fixed on the grain of the wooden table. "You're not the only one."

Jonathan took a slow sip of his whiskey. He had been wrestling with that same thought since his conversation with Bidzil.

"I spoke with the Chief's son a few days ago," Jonathan said, his voice quieter now. "He told me something that's been sitting with me ever since."

Ethan glanced up. "Yeah?"

Jonathan set his glass down, his fingers drumming lightly against the wooden table. "Bidzil told me he felt it inside him—the moment his father's spirit left the wolf."

Maria's expression softened. "Does he think the Chief has moved on?"

Jonathan nodded. "Yeah. And I think... maybe he did."

"And you don't believe it's merely coincidental?" Ethan asked.

Maria exhaled, shaking her head. "I don't think so. I think—" she paused as if weighing her words before speaking them aloud, "—the world has a balance to it. Maybe the Chief was part of that balance. Perhaps he was guiding us, protecting the land... even after he was gone."

Jonathan ran a hand through his beard, the coarse scruff still unfamiliar to him after years of being clean-shaven. "If you'd asked me a year ago, I would've told you that's a load of superstitious nonsense."

Maria looked at him. "And now?"

Jonathan glanced toward the window, where the mountains cradled the Greer Valley like a quiet guardian. "It seems I have a lot to learn."

Ethan sighed, shaking his head. "Well, you know what this means, right?"

Maria arched one brow. "What?"

Ethan lifted his glass with a dramatic flourish. "The spirits have personally blessed us, which means, effective immediately, I'm twenty percent funnier than when you first showed up."

Jonathan rolled his eyes. "You're making me age a decade every time you open your mouth."

Ethan smirked, crossing his arms. Then, with a perfectly straight face and a deep-voiced imitation of the Chief, he intoned, "Ha. Ha. Ha. You, Ethan, possess the humor of the spirits. They, too, suffer through your jokes."

Maria huffed, shaking her head, fighting back a laugh. "That is not what the Chief would say."

Ethan smirked. "No, but if he had my sense of humor, he would."

Maria rolled her eyes, but a smirk danced on her lips. "Good thing you're pretty because your mouth is insufferable."

Ethan leaned in slightly, his smirk deepening. "I am not pretty!"

Maria lifted her glass and took a slow sip while maintaining eye contact. "I think I need another drink."

Jonathan let out a long sigh. "I really should've sat at a different table."

The laughter that followed was warm and effortless, cutting through the weight of everything they had endured. For a moment, they weren't a retired game warden, a stubborn game warden, and a brilliant biologist. They were simply friends, sharing a meal, clinging to the lighter moments, aware of how quickly everything could be taken away.

After a moment, Jonathan set his whiskey down and cleared his throat. "We should toast."

Ethan arched a brow. "To what? My undeniable comedic genius?"

Maria smacked his arm. "To the Chief, idiot."

Ethan grinned, but his expression softened. He lifted his glass, and Maria followed.

Jonathan exhaled, raising his whiskey. His voice was soft. "To Chief Grey Cloud."

Their glasses met with a soft clink, the sound small but weighted with meaning.

The fire in the lobby crackled, wrapping its warmth throughout the bar. Outside, the mountains stood steadfast against the night.

And somewhere, out in the wild, a wolf moved through the trees.

***

By midday, Jonathan stood at the confluence of the Black River, where the East and West Forks merged, snaking through the rugged terrain like veins. The sun hung just past its peak, casting long golden streaks across the water. Nearby, an Apache Trout broke the surface, snatching a mayfly in a gentle ripple before vanishing into the current.

They had chosen this place carefully. A place where two paths converged, flowing forward as one.

The hill between the forks was gentle, sloping up from the water to provide a clear view downstream. It was a place of convergence, a place of connection- just as Bidzil now stepped into the role his father once held, bridging the past and the future.

At the heart of it all stood a sapling, its slender trunk bending gently in the breeze. It was a young ponderosa pine— related to the towering sentinels that had watched over this land for centuries, before any of them, before Chief Grey Cloud, long before even the oldest stories passed down by his ancestors.

Jonathan exhaled slowly, his fingers tightening around the worn wooden handle of the shovel beside him. His hands, hardened by years of labor, ached, and his knuckles were stiff with time, but this task felt right. He glanced at Ethan, Maria, and Bidzil, each silent and lost in their thoughts.

Bidzil was the first to step forward.

He knelt beside the sapling, resting a hand against its delicate trunk before reaching for a handful of soil. His fingers pressed into the earth, anchoring him to something deeper than the land.

"My father always told me the land remembers," he said, his voice steady but low. "What we do in this life, the way we treat the earth, the way we walk upon it—it lingers. It echoes through time."

He let the soil fall gently over the roots.

"I want to honor him not just with this tree but with the way I serve. The way I protect what he loved." He exhaled, pressing the soil down lightly before stepping back.

Jonathan observed the young man, noting his build and quiet determination in his stance. With a subtle nod to himself, he then stepped forward.

The shovel felt heavier in his grip than it ought to have, or perhaps that was just age creeping in. He pressed the blade into the soil, lifting the damp earth and allowing it to fall gently over the roots.

"Your father taught me things I never thought I needed to learn," Jonathan admitted, his voice rougher than he intended.

He paused, clearing his throat before continuing. "I spent my whole life believing I understood these mountains. I knew the trails, the rivers, the way the seasons shaped the land. But he revealed something else—something deeper. A way of seeing beyond the physical."

He pressed the soil into place with his boot, patting the mound with the flat edge of the shovel.

"That's something I will never forget."

Stepping back, he handed the shovel to Ethan.

Ethan, who always carried himself with ease, now appeared more serious. He gazed at the sapling for a long moment before crouching down, letting his fingers sift through the loose earth.

"I don't know much about spirits," he admitted, his voice quieter than usual. "But I know a good man when I meet one."

He let the soil fall through his fingers.

"The Chief saw the world as it should be, not just as it was. And I think… that's rare." He shook his head, his upper lip starting to twitch. "I'd like to be more like that."

He brushed the dirt from his palms and stepped away.

Maria was the last. She stood still for a moment with her arms crossed as if gathering her thoughts. When she finally moved, it was with quiet purpose.

"I grew up believing in science. In fact, numbers, data. I still do," she said, kneeling beside the sapling. "But this place…

these mountains… they make you feel something. Something that can't be researched or proven with data points."

She traced her fingers along the young tree's bark before gathering a handful of soil in her palm.

"I think the Chief understood that balance. The way science and spirit—knowledge and belief—can exist together." She pressed the soil into place. "I understand it better now."

For a moment, no one spoke.

Suddenly, a gust of wind swept through the trees, rustling the branches above, tugging at the loose strands of Maria's braids, and lifting the dust at their feet into a swirling dust devil.

Jonathan looked up.

In the distance, a herd of wild horses drank from the Black River. Upon noticing them, the horses lifted their heads and swiftly trotted up the hillside.

Bidzil closed his eyes, tilting his head slightly as if listening to something only he could hear.

Jonathan let out a slow breath.

Some endings aren't endings at all.

They were merely the beginning.

As the last of the soil settled around the young tree's roots, Jonathan knew without a doubt—that Chief Grey Cloud would always be here.

***

Later that evening, the trio invited Bidzil to join them for dinner. It was a way to savor the moment a little longer before they all returned to their respective duties. However, throughout the meal, Bidzil remained unusually quiet.

Jonathan noticed it first—the way he observed them, his dark eyes shifting between their faces as they spoke, absorbing every word. He wasn't merely hearing them; he was truly listening.

It was in the way Maria spoke about the balance between science and spirit, wrestling with things she couldn't quantify. Likewise, Ethan, ever the skeptic, admitted that the Chief saw the world not just as it was but as it should be. And Jonathan, well… he had spent years believing he understood these mountains, only for the Chief to reveal something deeper to him.

By the time they finished their drinks and departed from the warm glow of the restaurant, Bidzil had made up his mind.

"I want to take you somewhere," he said simply.

Jonathan met his gaze, recognizing something in it. Something unshaken.

Without another word, they followed him.

***

They drove deep into the Apache reservation, following a winding dirt road that stretched endlessly into the wilderness. As they climbed higher, the air turned crisp, and the Douglas firs began to appear, revealing grassy meadows below.

The Chief's final resting place.

When they stepped out of the truck, Bidzil led them toward a flat outcrop of rock, where the land fell away into a vast expanse. A massive rock formation, weathered by time, jutted from the ridge—its shape unmistakably resembling that of an eagle's head, watching over the land below. Beneath it, etched into the stone, lay the petroglyphs of their ancestors—stories carved into the earth, preserving the legacy for future generations.

"This place was sacred to him," Bidzil said at last.

Jonathan glanced around. He understood why. It wasn't just beautiful; it was untouched. A place where a man could sit and watch the world without feeling as if time was chasing him down.

Bidzil exhaled, crouching beside a small pile of stones—a marker placed deliberately among the earth. His fingers lightly brushed over them before he spoke.

"My father once told me that Mother Nature remembers." Bidzil's voice was steady yet tinged with something deeper. "No matter what we build or destroy, the land retains everything. And in time, it will respond to how we treat it."

He turned his gaze toward the distant mountains. "He was from the Bear Clan. Nagodishgizh'n. He taught me the old ways: how to listen to the land, read the signs in the wind and animals, and understand how the water moves."

Bidzil paused, his fingers tracing the edge of one of the stones. "But the last thing he ever told me was that leadership isn't about holding power; it's about serving others. And from that, the land will heal you."

Jonathan felt his throat tighten.

Slowly, he knelt down. Reaching into his jacket pocket, he pulled out a small, smooth stone that he had carried for days, uncertain of the reason why.

He placed it gently beside the others.

Maria tilted her head. "Where's it from?"

"Milk Creek," Jonathan murmured.

Ethan's brow furrowed, but then he seemed to understand. "The last grizzly."

Jonathan nodded. "The last grizzly in Arizona was shot there." He exhaled, settling back on his heels. "But now... they're back. Mother Nature responded."

Bidzil studied the stone for a moment before giving a solemn nod.

Then, a solitary hawk soared overhead, its wings slicing through the dimming light. It uttered a piercing cry, echoing through the sky before disappearing into the horizon.

"Some spirits never leave," Bidzil said quietly. "They just become part of the wild."

XIII: The White Elk

Maria leaned over her desk, her fingers moving swiftly across the keyboard as data filled the screen—population numbers, tracking logs, and field reports. Beside her, a large map of eastern Arizona and New Mexico hung on a corkboard adorned with red and blue pins, indicating pack territories, dispersions, and den sites of the Mexican Grey Wolf.

The department felt quiet, punctuated only by the occasional hum of printers and the faint murmur of distant conversations from the break room. The rich aroma of coffee and office supplies lingered in the air. Behind her, a row of GPS-enabled collars rested neatly on the shelf next to a stack of freshly printed reports.

Maria adjusted her glasses and scrolled through the latest population data, her eyes fixed on the monitor.

"Two hundred and eighty-six," she murmured, more to herself than anyone else.

"Amazing."

Ethan's voice came from behind her, carrying a hint of distraction; however, Maria had learned that this was often intentional with him.

She turned briefly and found him leaning against the doorframe, arms crossed, wearing the expression of someone who had just gotten away with a crime. His sleeves were rolled up, and his look made it clear that he wasn't interested in a conversation about population numbers.

Maria barely looked up before returning her gaze to the screen, unfazed. "Two hundred eighty-six wolves in Arizona and New Mexico. One hundred sixty-four pups were born in 2024, with a 48% survival rate. Ethan, the population has grown for nine consecutive years!"

Ethan let out a low whistle, pushing away from the doorframe as he walked into the room. "Sounds like a reason to celebrate – champagne and dinner? What do you think?"

Maria grabbed a thick manila folder from her desk and smacked it against his arm as he walked by. "Dinner? Maybe I should report you to HR for flirting on the job?" she teased, flashing a smile and adding a wink. "But seriously, I'm so proud of this team and all the agencies involved. We've exceeded both our genetic and demographic goals this year."

Unfazed, Ethan dramatically rubbed his arm while sitting on the edge of her desk. "I'm talking about a *romantic* dinner."

Maria sighed as she flipped through a stack of tracking reports. "Ethan, you wouldn't recognize romance even if it walked up and recited a Shakespearean sonnet."

Ethan grinned. "You seriously underestimate my talents."

Maria didn't bother looking up. "Mhm. Sure. Anyway."

She gathered a stack of documents and headed toward the filing cabinet in the corner, unaware of Ethan's subtle attempt to brush his hand against hers.

He sighed when she moved away, shaking his head. "Are you ignoring me?"

Maria opened the filing drawer, scanning through the tabs. "You are definitely not being ignored. You're standing right there."

Ethan laughed. "Crazy to think how many people doubted free-ranging wolves would survive in Arizona. I mean, we're not far from a full recovery now."

Maria retrieved another folder, flipping it open as she returned to her desk. "It's amazing. I'm even more surprised that the fostering efforts have been so successful. As of today, we have twenty fostered pups, and all have reached breeding age."

She flipped the folder over, revealing images of wolves captured on game cameras. Some wore bright green collars, while others navigated through the underbrush with pups trailing behind them.

"About fifty percent are collared," she continued, "meaning at least two wolves per pack have tracking devices. That's our safety net—if one signal is lost, we still have another wolf in the same territory."

Ethan leaned closer, pretending to study the images, but was undoubtedly trying to regain her attention.

"Right, right," he muttered. "Have dinner with me tonight. We talk all about wolves. Packs. Lone Wolves. Breeding Rituals."

Maria raised an eyebrow, unimpressed by the innuendo. "Wow, Ethan. Nothing sets a mood like a deep dive into wolf breeding. Check this out."

She clicked on one of the collar signals and pointed to the screen. "The Elk Horn pack has extended its territory. You remember them?"

Ethan blinked, looking at the map. "The ones near Escudilla Mountain?"

"Exactly." Maria nodded. "We now have three pups that were cross-fostered into this pack with two collared males."

Ethan rubbed his chin, abandoning his attempt at flirting, and started to focus. "So, this means you can track this pack more accurately now?"

Maria nodded, "Exactly. It also lets us track their interactions with other packs, monitor prey availability, and see how close they are getting to humans."

Ethan watched her work for a moment, his expression shifting into a proud smile.

"I love how much you love your job," he said.

Maria met his gaze and saw him for the first time since he walked in.

"I do," she admitted. "Because it's working. The numbers prove it." She exhaled, looking back at the data. "Wins like this don't come often for wildlife."

Ethan nodded. "Here's to 2025 being a step in the right direction." He raised an imaginary glass with a grin.

Maria tapped the screen for emphasis. "One step closer to wild hearts running free."

Ethan raised an eyebrow, amused. "That was poetic! Am I finally starting to rub off on you?"

Maria smirked, grabbing a report and tossing it onto his lap. "Keep dreaming."

Ethan chuckled, shaking his head as he picked up the file. "You know, for a scientist, you have no sense of romance at all."

Maria smirked. "I save my passion for things that actually matter."

Ethan grinned. "I'd be offended if I wasn't so damn impressed."

Maria sat across from him, finally relaxing as she leaned her elbow on the desk. "I'll take that as a compliment."

"Yes, I will go to dinner with you tonight," she said.

Ethan blinked, briefly taken aback before a slow, genuine smile spread across his face. "You have no idea how happy I am."

He watched her for a moment longer, absorbing the determination in her eyes and the fire behind every word she spoke. She wasn't just brilliant; she was relentless and passionate, the kind of person who improved the world by caring enough to fight for it.

And damn, did he appreciate her for it.

***

The warm murmur of conversation, the twang of George Strait's '*Amarillo by Morning*' drifting from the Bluetooth speaker behind the bar, and the bustling crowd of locals and desert tourists all contributed to the welcoming atmosphere of Molly Butler's.

Jonathan leaned back in his chair, rolling his whiskey glass between his fingers as he watched Ethan grinning as if he had just won a carnival prize.

"Alright, go on," Jonathan muttered. "Whatever it is, just say it already. You two have been exchanging looks like two teenagers ditching prom night."

Ethan flashed a broad grin and playfully nudged Maria. She rolled her eyes, but her subsequent smirk didn't go unnoticed.

"Well," Ethan drawled. "Since you asked so nicely, we have some news."

Maria, still amused, reached for her beer bottle and took a slow sip before finally indulging him. "We're moving in together."

Jonathan arched a brow, then exhaled a slow chuckle, shaking his head. "I'll be damned. What took so long?"

Ethan placed a hand over his heart, pretending to be offended. "You think I've been dragging my feet? She's made me work for this!"

Jonathan snorted. "I mention that because she truly possesses common sense."

Maria smirked, clearly pleased. "Told you he'd take my side."

Ethan leaned back, unbothered. "Common sense is overrated."

Jonathan took a slow sip of whiskey, giving him a scrutinizing look. "You hardly qualify for this relationship. I'm still trying to understand how you managed it."

Ethan exhaled through his nose, clearly prepared. "Well, see, the thing is—"

Maria cut him off with a pat on his shoulder. "Don't embarrass yourself."

Jonathan huffed a laugh, setting his glass down with a soft thunk. "Smart woman."

Ethan put on a grand show of sighing, yet he couldn't erase the grin from his face.

The waitress approached their table and placed their plates down. It was a glorious sight of seared ribeye, mashed potatoes smothered in Mormon gravy, and a side of steamed vegetables.

"Anything else for you guys?" she asked, smiling.

Ethan glanced at Jonathan. "Another round, yeah?"

Jonathan nodded in approval, and Maria, ever the responsible one, smirked. "I'm cutting you off after two."

Ethan placed a hand over hers on the table, feigning drama. "You keep me *so grounded.*"

Jonathan chuckled into his drink.

The night flowed with easy conversation as the three slipped effortlessly into their familiar rhythm. There was something about the afterglow of good news—a sense that, just for a moment, the world was in a good place.

Just as Jonathan sipped his second drink, two men entered the bar, their steel-toed work boots scuffing against the wooden floor.

Jonathan glanced up as Nakai, the Ski Patrol Director at Sunrise Ski Resort, spotted him and flashed a wide, toothy grin.

"Crow!" Nakai's deep voice cut through the low hum of the bar.

Jonathan pushed his chair back and stood up, his joints protesting slightly, but his expression remained warm. "Nakai," he said, gripping the man's hand firmly.

Nakai was broad-shouldered, with short black hair feathered to one side and features sharp and weathered from years spent in the high-altitude cold. His companion, a younger Apache man, offered Jonathan a polite nod before taking a seat at the bar.

Nakai slapped Jonathan on the shoulder before pulling up a chair at their table.

"Didn't expect to see you here," Jonathan said, settling back into his seat.

Nakai shrugged. "Figured I owed you a drink after everything you've done." His expression softened slightly. "And... I wanted to celebrate the Chief."

Jonathan nodded, the mention of Chief Grey Cloud adding a familiar weight to the moment. He raised his glass in tribute. "To the Chief."

Nakai exhaled, resting his arms on the table. "I know it's been a few months, but the land feels empty without him."

Jonathan tapped a finger lightly against his whiskey glass. "It does."

At that moment, an unspoken understanding passed between them. They shared the loss of a leader, a mentor, and a man who had been a pillar of the White Mountains for decades.

Ethan leaned back in his chair, giving them a moment – but in true Ethan fashion, he couldn't resist jumping in.

"So, Nakai," he said, drumming his fingers on the table. "When are you gonna convince this old man to join ski patrol?"

Maria closed her eyes briefly, sighing through her nose. "Oh no."

Nakai grinned. "That's a good question." He turned to Jonathan with an encouraging look. "Let's get you through training, and you'll be pulling a toboggan by winter!"

Jonathan let out a dry laugh. "I'd rather a Kodiak grizzly pole vault onto my body!"

Ethan, grinning, crossed his arms. "I mean, come on, Crow. What's stopping you?"

Jonathan deadpanned. "My knees."

Maria choked on her drink, coughing out a laugh.

Ethan, unfazed, waved a hand. "We'll get you some fancy knee braces. Besides, ski poles are like crutches anyway, right?"

Nakai chuckled. "Hey, the offer's always there. We could use a guy who knows these mountains the way you do."

Jonathan leaned back in his chair, shaking his head. "I'll think about it. And by that, I mean I'll never do it."

Nakai grinned. "Duly noted. I'll ask you again when the snow comes."

They sat there a while longer, sharing drinks, swapping stories, and allowing the weight of the past to transform into something lighter.

Outside, the mountains beyond the meadow stood silent, their rolling peaks illuminated by the moon's glow.

For a fleeting moment, everything felt right.

Then, like all moments, it passed.

Jonathan noticed a change in Nakai's expression. The humor had vanished—replaced by something more cutting than the usual playful teasing about his knees. His features became taut, and his typically relaxed posture stiffened as he gazed out one of the windows.

Jonathan followed his gaze but saw nothing unusual—only a rancher assisting a tourist in jump-starting their vehicle after they had left their lights on.

Ethan noticed it, too. He leaned forward, elbows on the table, his grin fading. "Something on your mind?"

Nakai kept his gaze fixed on the window, his fingers lightly tapping against the wooden table. His voice was quieter now, more profound. "Yeah. Something is coming."

Jonathan had known Nakai long enough to recognize that he wasn't merely succumbing to superstition. He set his whiskey glass down and met his gaze. "Care to be a bit more specific?"

Nakai hesitated for just a moment, then looked between them. "We were clearing trees yesterday. Backside of Apache Mountain."

Jonathan already had a feeling where this was headed.

Nakai leaned in slightly. "We spotted an albino elk."

Maria, who had been listening quietly, sat up straighter, her brow furrowing. "An albino elk?" she echoed. "That's incredibly rare."

"Rare enough that I've only seen one other in my life," Nakai confirmed. "And I've spent all my days in these mountains."

Maria stared at her glass, deep in thought. "Albinism in elk is extremely rare. The chances of one surviving to adulthood? Even lower. Most don't make it past calfhood – they're too easy for predators to spot." She exhaled, her fingers tracing the rim of her glass. "But if it was fully grown…"

"It was," Nakai said firmly, "a seven-by-seven bull. Trophy-sized."

Ethan raised an eyebrow, maintaining a casual tone. "Sounds like an incredible sight. So, why are you acting like we won't be getting any snow this winter?"

Nakai didn't smile. "Because it's not just a sighting. In our tradition, an albino elk is an omen. A warning."

Jonathan was familiar with these beliefs. He had spent years in these mountains, observing men like Chief Grey Cloud interpret the land as if it were a relative.

Ethan, however, wasn't one to take things at face value.

"A warning about what?" he questioned.

Nakai shook his head. "I don't know yet. But when an albino elk appears, it's never without reason." He looked at Jonathan then, his gaze steady. "You know that."

Jonathan didn't respond right away. He felt Ethan's attention on him, waiting to see if he would dismiss it or acknowledge something deeper.

After a moment, Jonathan leaned back in his chair, exhaling slowly through his nose. "When the land sends you a message," he said simply, "you listen."

Maria glanced back and forth between them, her expression thoughtful. "Perhaps we shouldn't overlook it."

Their plates were empty, with only a smear of Mormon gravy left behind. Maria picked up her beer bottle, lost in thought. Ethan had grown quiet, his usual relaxed energy subdued.

Jonathan wasn't saying much, either.

For a few minutes, the only sound was the steady murmur of voices in the bar as the speaker behind the bar played 'Ghost Riders in the Sky. ' Its eerie, haunting melody added a chill to the moment.

Then, without warning, the lights went dark.

The room appeared to hold its breath as the lights began to flicker, their warm glow pulsating before stabilizing. A cold gust of wind rattled the windows, making the glass shudder in its frames.

A few people glanced up from their tables, whispering to one another.

Ethan looked up at the ceiling. "Well, that's a little ominous."

Jonathan turned his gaze toward the windows. "Storm coming?"

Nakai shook his head. "Nothing in the forecast."

Maria pulled her sweater tighter around her shoulders, feeling a chill wrap around her body. Outside, the wind picked up, causing the trees to sway in the darkness.

Then—

A child's sharp gasp cut through the quiet.

"Daddy, look! It's a ghost!"

The whole bar appeared to turn toward the little boy, his tiny hands pressed against the window, his breath fogging the glass as he pointed toward the riverbank beyond the lodge.

Jonathan felt his stomach tighten.

He pushed back his chair and stood up, walking toward the window. Ethan and Maria followed quietly.

Outside, beneath the pale glow of the moon, something stirred.

A shape—tall, powerful, and strikingly white against the darkened landscape.

Jonathan's breath stopped.

An albino elk appeared along the Little Colorado River, its massive antlers shining in the dim light, its ghostly form barely discernible against the darkened landscape.

Maria exhaled slowly. "That's... unbelievable."

Nakai's jaw was tense, his hands at his sides as he watched. "Believe it." His voice was low. "Something is coming."

The elk paused, its large, dark eyes fixed on them through the window as if it sensed it was being watched.

Then, as suddenly as it had appeared, it slipped into the willows, disappearing into the darkness.

Jonathan's pulse remained steady, his breath calm – but deep in his gut, something churned. He knew it then.

This wasn't over.

Not yet.

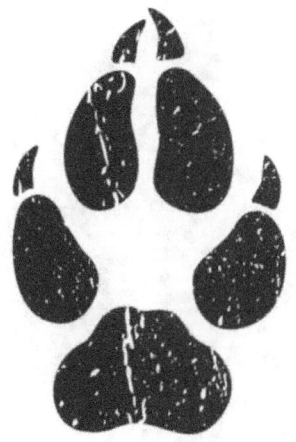

www.ingramcontent.com/pod-product-compliance
Lightning Source LLC
Chambersburg PA
CBHW060421260626
47161CB00005B/1734